RISE OF THE OCEAN GOD

Story by
Sebastian Girner

Art by
Ray-Anthony Height
Nate Lovett

MONSUNO: COMBAT CHAOS
Volume 3
RISE OF THE OCEAN GOD

Story by Sebastian Girner
Art by Ray-Anthony Height & Nate Lovett
Letters by Zack Turner

Design/Sam Elzway
Editor/Joel Enos

Printed in China

Published by VIZ Media, LLC
P.O. Box 77010
San Francisco, CA 94107

10 9 8 7 6 5 4 3 2 1
First printing, December 2013

VOLUME 3
RISE OF THE OCEAN GOD

TABLE OF CONTENTS

CHARACTERS

CHASE & LOCK

Chase is on a quest to both find his missing father, the scientist who discovered Monsuno, and figure out a way for humans and Monsuno to coexist peacefully. He's learning how to be the hero that he needs to be to make that happen. Chase's Monsuno, the powerful and loyal Lock, was left for him by his father.

BREN & QUICKFORCE

Chase's best friend since childhood. He is a fast-talking genius, but he lacks courage. Bren's loyal Monsuno is the volatile Quickforce.

JINJA & CHARGER

The unpredictable Jinja has no patience for bad guys. She's quick to act and even quicker to tell you if you're wrong! Her Monsuno is the tough-skinned Charger.

BEYAL & GLOWBLADE

Beyal is a mystic monk who would rather meditate than fight. He has a strong spiritual connection to Monsuno that none of his friends have yet developed. Beyal's Monsuno, Glowblade, is a scorpion-like reptile that is always ready to strike at its master's command.

DAX & AIRSWITCH

Dax is the rebel of the team. His act-first-think-later attitude sometimes gets him and his clawed Monsuno, Airswitch, into trouble.

DR. KLIPSE

The main villain in the Monsuno story. He wants to control the world by demolishing society and creating a new world order where he rules with the power of Monsuno. His Monsuno of choice is the terribly scary Backslash.

DR. MOTO

Her secret experiments with Monsuno got out of hand, then she went into hiding. But maybe not for as long as the team hopes!

HARGRAVE

Dr. Klipse's loyal butler is full of creepy secrets.

THE STORY OF
MONSUNO

65 MILLION YEARS AGO – Meteors fell to Earth carrying life-forms made out of powerful, chaotic, uncontrollable genetic material. This was the Monsuno—origin unknown and the real reason why the dinosaurs became extinct! Soon after, the Monsuno essence fell dormant and stayed that way for millions of years...until...

TODAY – A potent energy source is discovered in the K-layers of the planet. Scientist Jeredy Suno believes he's found a solution to the ever-mounting energy crisis. But what he doesn't know is that this green energy source is a ticking time bomb!

Dr. Suno's research breakthrough could be used to benefit all mankind. But the awakened Monsuno essence could also potentially wipe out humans like it did the dinosaurs!

When Dr. Suno goes missing, his 15-year-old son, Chase, ventures out to find him. Chase discovers the power of Monsuno, and now he and his friends are in an all-out race for survival against dangerous villains seeking power and a secret government agency seeking control of the most powerful creatures ever known...the Monsuno!

MONSUNO® COMBAT CHAOS™

RISE OF THE OCEAN GOD

Chapter 1: The Professor

FLASH

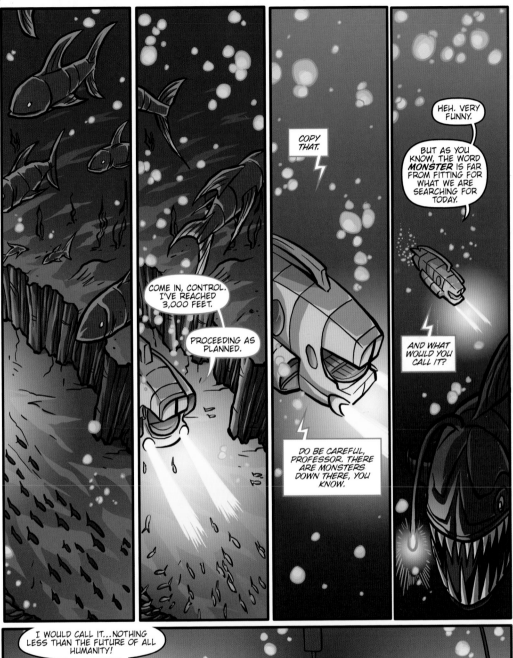

COME IN, CONTROL. I'VE REACHED 3,000 FEET.

PROCEEDING AS PLANNED.

COPY THAT.

DO BE CAREFUL, PROFESSOR. THERE ARE MONSTERS DOWN THERE, YOU KNOW.

HEH. VERY FUNNY.

BUT AS YOU KNOW, THE WORD *MONSTER* IS FAR FROM FITTING FOR WHAT WE ARE SEARCHING FOR TODAY.

AND WHAT WOULD YOU CALL IT?

I WOULD CALL IT...NOTHING LESS THAN THE FUTURE OF ALL HUMANITY!

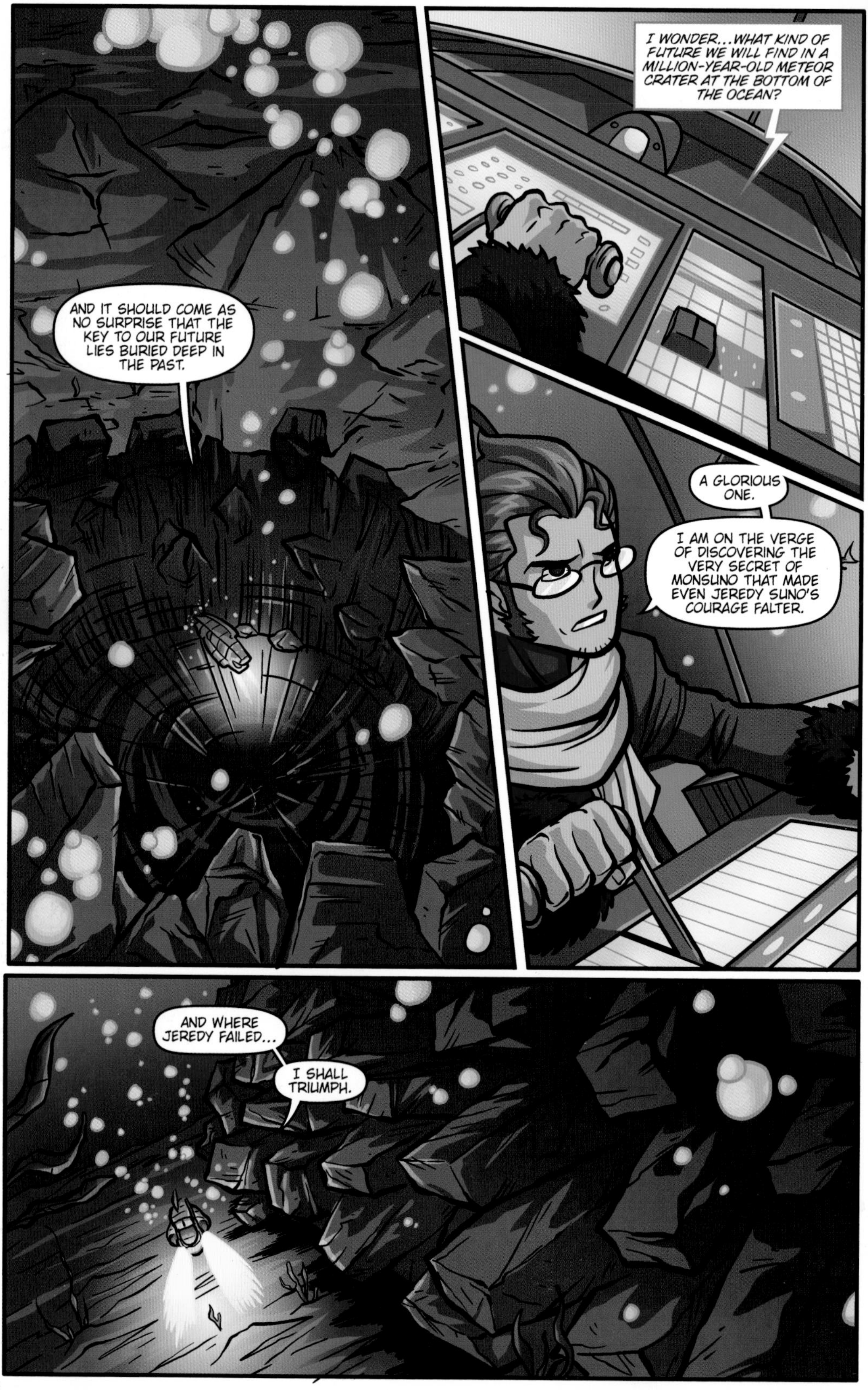
I WONDER...WHAT KIND OF FUTURE WE WILL FIND IN A MILLION-YEAR-OLD METEOR CRATER AT THE BOTTOM OF THE OCEAN?
AND IT SHOULD COME AS NO SURPRISE THAT THE KEY TO OUR FUTURE LIES BURIED DEEP IN THE PAST.
A GLORIOUS ONE.
I AM ON THE VERGE OF DISCOVERING THE VERY SECRET OF MONSUNO THAT MADE EVEN JEREDY SUNO'S COURAGE FALTER.
AND WHERE JEREDY FAILED...
I SHALL TRIUMPH.

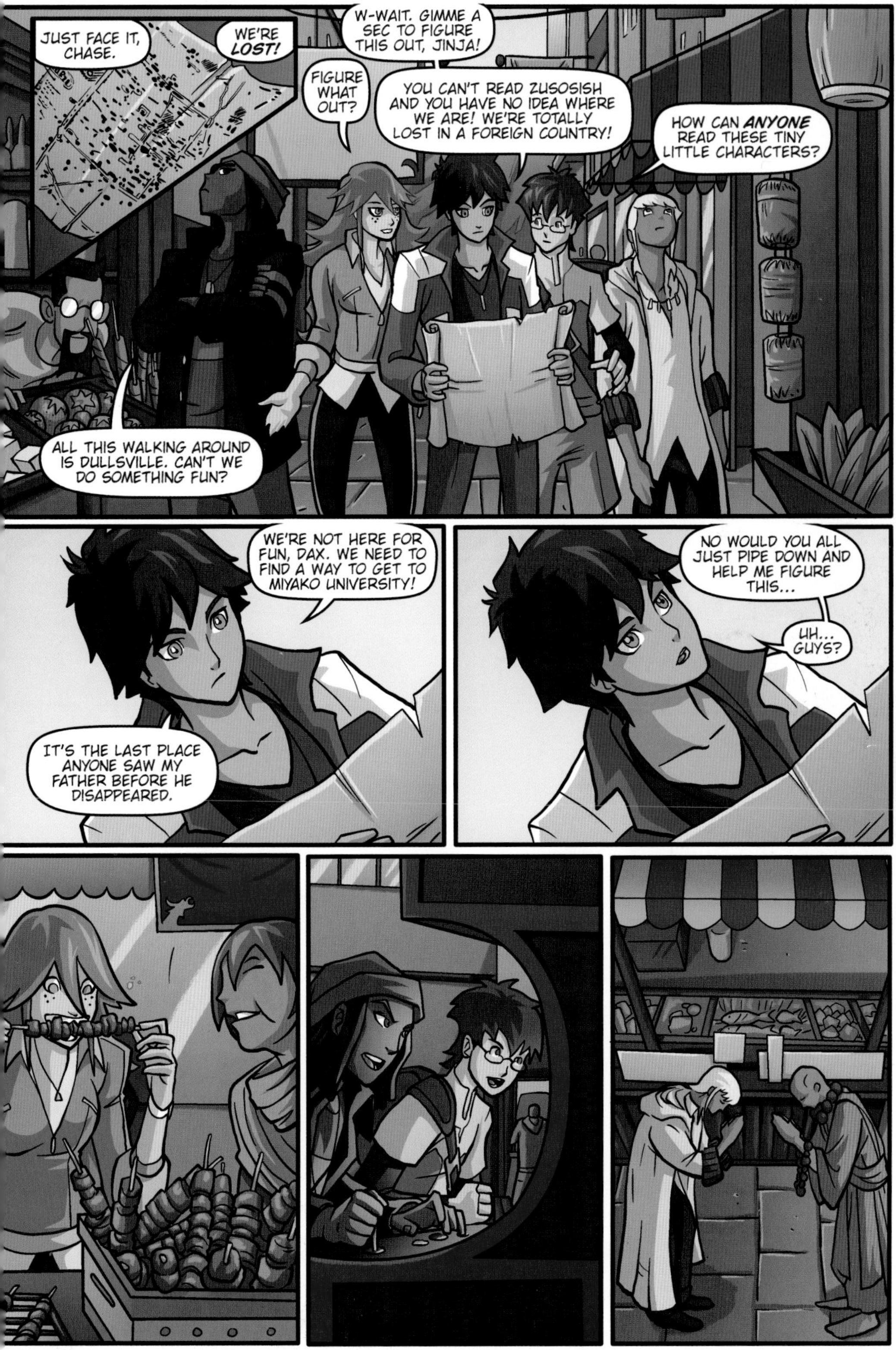
JUST FACE IT, CHASE.
WE'RE *LOST!*
W-WAIT. GIMME A SEC TO FIGURE THIS OUT, JINJA!
FIGURE WHAT OUT?
YOU CAN'T READ ZUSOSISH AND YOU HAVE NO IDEA WHERE WE ARE! WE'RE TOTALLY LOST IN A FOREIGN COUNTRY!
HOW CAN *ANYONE* READ THESE TINY LITTLE CHARACTERS?
ALL THIS WALKING AROUND IS DULLSVILLE. CAN'T WE DO SOMETHING FUN?
WE'RE NOT HERE FOR FUN, DAX. WE NEED TO FIND A WAY TO GET TO MIYAKO UNIVERSITY!
IT'S THE LAST PLACE ANYONE SAW MY FATHER BEFORE HE DISAPPEARED.
NO WOULD YOU ALL JUST PIPE DOWN AND HELP ME FIGURE THIS...
UH... GUYS?

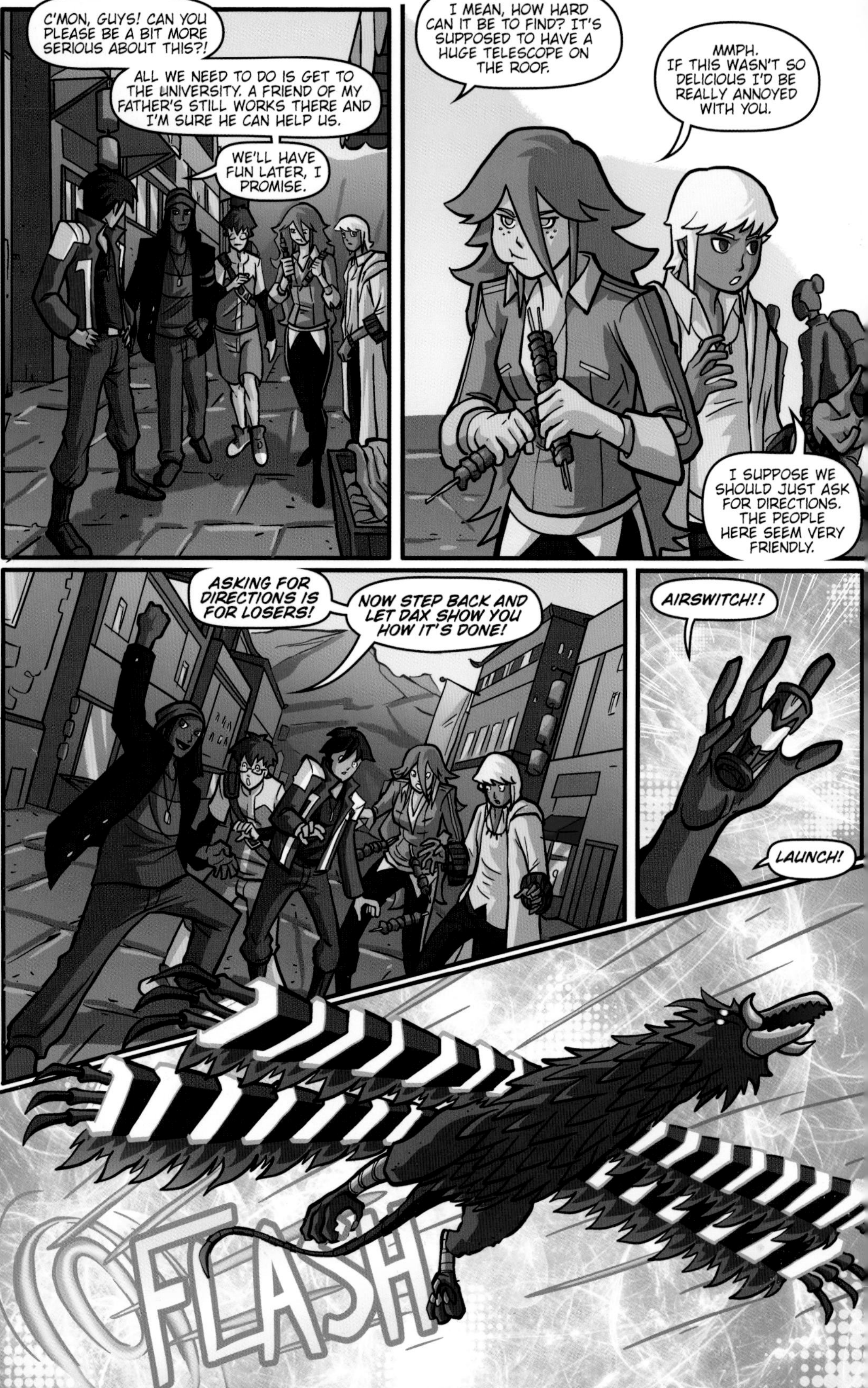
C'MON, GUYS! CAN YOU PLEASE BE A BIT MORE SERIOUS ABOUT THIS?!
ALL WE NEED TO DO IS GET TO THE UNIVERSITY. A FRIEND OF MY FATHER'S STILL WORKS THERE AND I'M SURE HE CAN HELP US.
WE'LL HAVE FUN LATER, I PROMISE.
I MEAN, HOW HARD CAN IT BE TO FIND? IT'S SUPPOSED TO HAVE A HUGE TELESCOPE ON THE ROOF.
MMPH. IF THIS WASN'T SO DELICIOUS I'D BE REALLY ANNOYED WITH YOU.
I SUPPOSE WE SHOULD JUST ASK FOR DIRECTIONS. THE PEOPLE HERE SEEM VERY FRIENDLY.
ASKING FOR DIRECTIONS IS FOR LOSERS!
NOW STEP BACK AND LET DAX SHOW YOU HOW IT'S DONE!
AIRSWITCH!!
LAUNCH!
FLASH

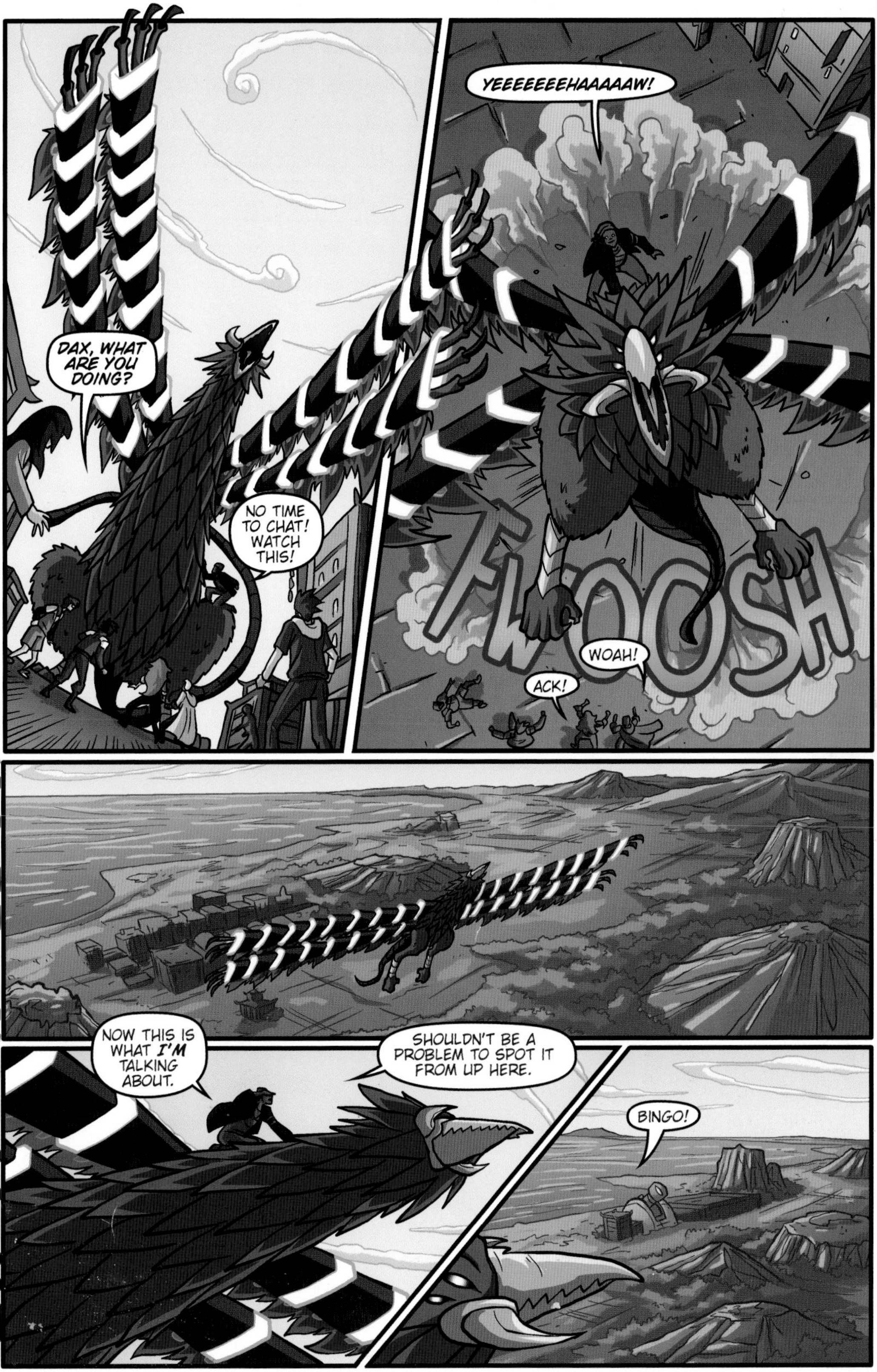
YEEEEEEEHAAAAAW!
DAX, WHAT ARE YOU DOING?
NO TIME TO CHAT! WATCH THIS!
FWOOSH
WOAH!
ACK!
NOW THIS IS WHAT *I'M* TALKING ABOUT.
SHOULDN'T BE A PROBLEM TO SPOT IT FROM UP HERE.
BINGO!

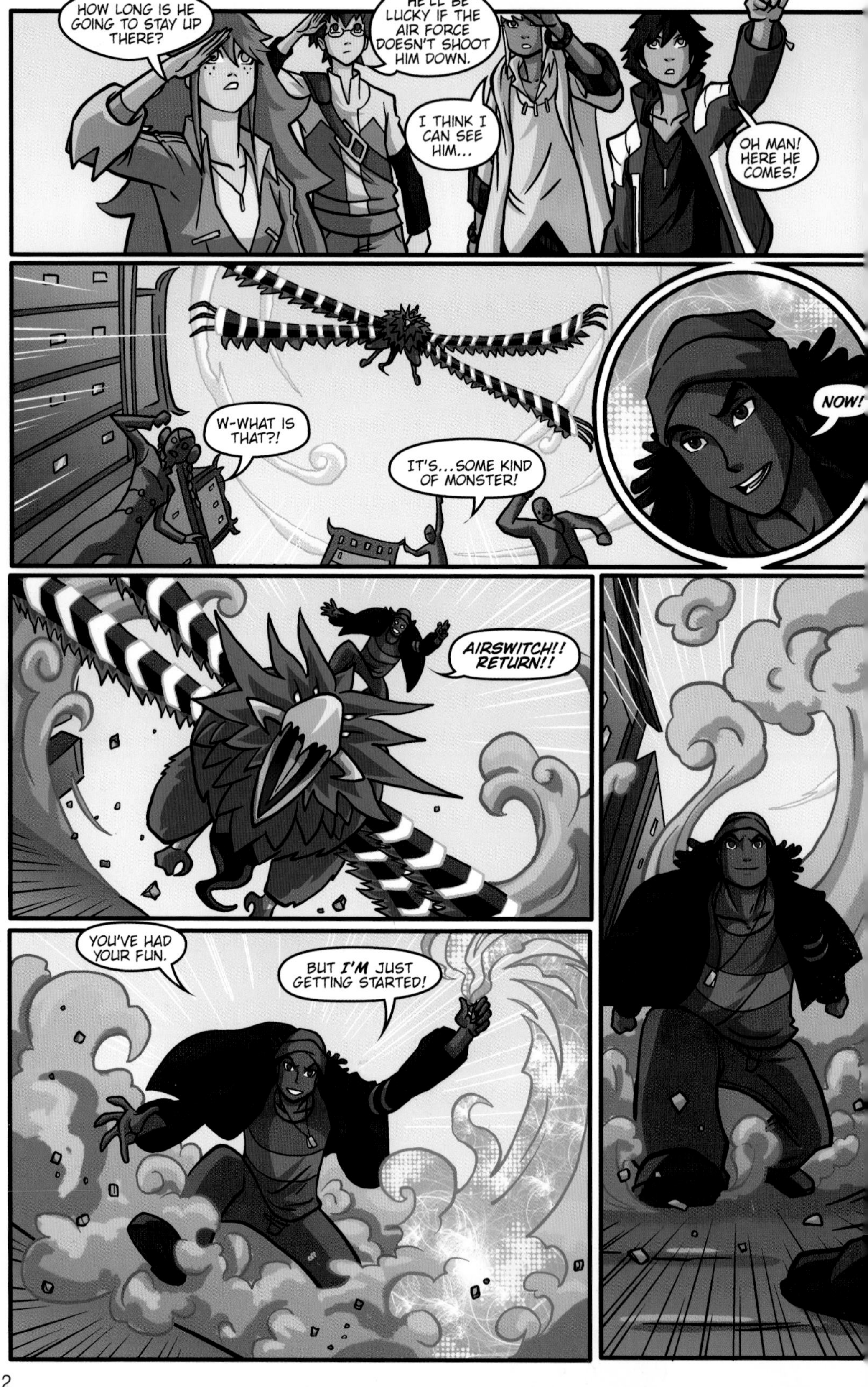
HOW LONG IS HE GOING TO STAY UP THERE?
HE'LL BE LUCKY IF THE AIR FORCE DOESN'T SHOOT HIM DOWN.
I THINK I CAN SEE HIM...
OH MAN! HERE HE COMES!
W-WHAT IS THAT?!
IT'S...SOME KIND OF MONSTER!
NOW!
AIRSWITCH!! RETURN!!
YOU'VE HAD YOUR FUN.
BUT ***I'M*** JUST GETTING STARTED!

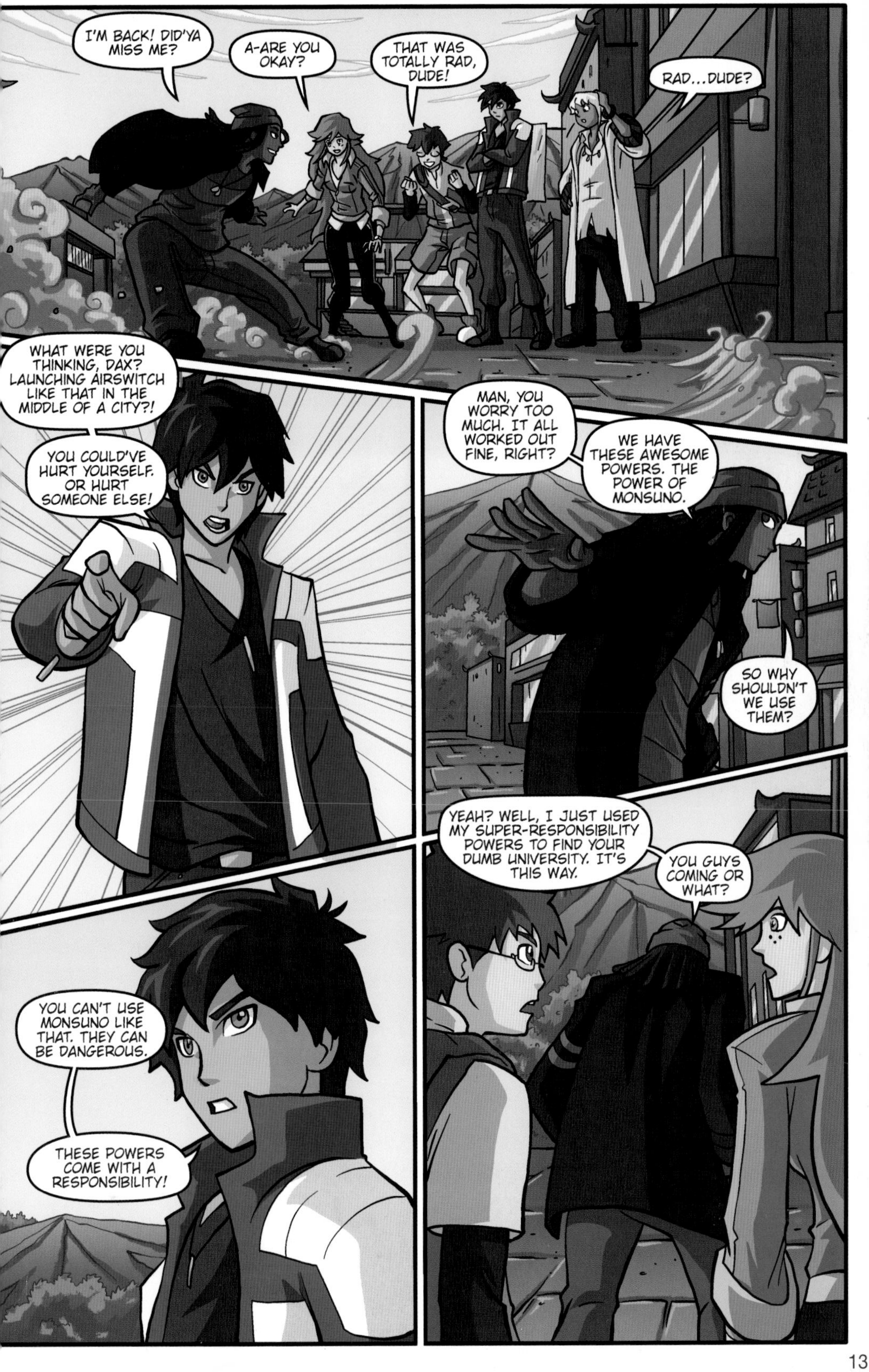
I'M BACK! DID'YA MISS ME?
A-ARE YOU OKAY?
THAT WAS TOTALLY RAD, DUDE!
RAD...DUDE?
WHAT WERE YOU THINKING, DAX? LAUNCHING AIRSWITCH LIKE THAT IN THE MIDDLE OF A CITY?!
YOU COULD'VE HURT YOURSELF. OR HURT SOMEONE ELSE!
MAN, YOU WORRY TOO MUCH. IT ALL WORKED OUT FINE, RIGHT?
WE HAVE THESE AWESOME POWERS. THE POWER OF MONSUNO.
SO WHY SHOULDN'T WE USE THEM?
YOU CAN'T USE MONSUNO LIKE THAT. THEY CAN BE DANGEROUS.
THESE POWERS COME WITH A RESPONSIBILITY!
YEAH? WELL, I JUST USED MY SUPER-RESPONSIBILITY POWERS TO FIND YOUR DUMB UNIVERSITY. IT'S THIS WAY.
YOU GUYS COMING OR WHAT?

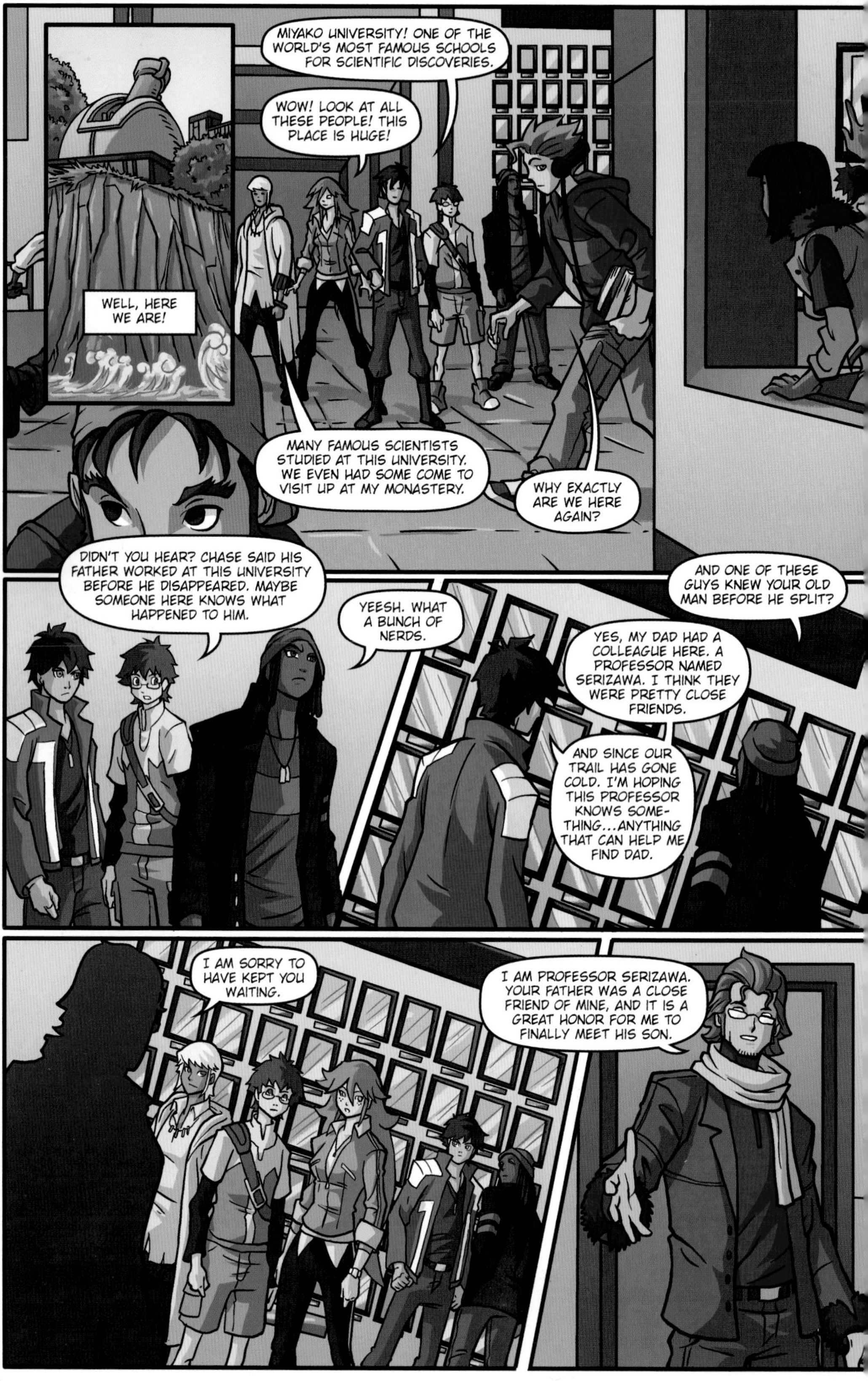
WELL, HERE WE ARE!
MIYAKO UNIVERSITY! ONE OF THE WORLD'S MOST FAMOUS SCHOOLS FOR SCIENTIFIC DISCOVERIES.
WOW! LOOK AT ALL THESE PEOPLE! THIS PLACE IS HUGE!
MANY FAMOUS SCIENTISTS STUDIED AT THIS UNIVERSITY. WE EVEN HAD SOME COME TO VISIT UP AT MY MONASTERY.
WHY EXACTLY ARE WE HERE AGAIN?
DIDN'T YOU HEAR? CHASE SAID HIS FATHER WORKED AT THIS UNIVERSITY BEFORE HE DISAPPEARED. MAYBE SOMEONE HERE KNOWS WHAT HAPPENED TO HIM.
YEESH. WHAT A BUNCH OF NERDS.
AND ONE OF THESE GUYS KNEW YOUR OLD MAN BEFORE HE SPLIT?
YES, MY DAD HAD A COLLEAGUE HERE. A PROFESSOR NAMED SERIZAWA. I THINK THEY WERE PRETTY CLOSE FRIENDS.
AND SINCE OUR TRAIL HAS GONE COLD, I'M HOPING THIS PROFESSOR KNOWS SOME-THING...ANYTHING THAT CAN HELP ME FIND DAD.
I AM SORRY TO HAVE KEPT YOU WAITING.
I AM PROFESSOR SERIZAWA. YOUR FATHER WAS A CLOSE FRIEND OF MINE, AND IT IS A GREAT HONOR FOR ME TO FINALLY MEET HIS SON.

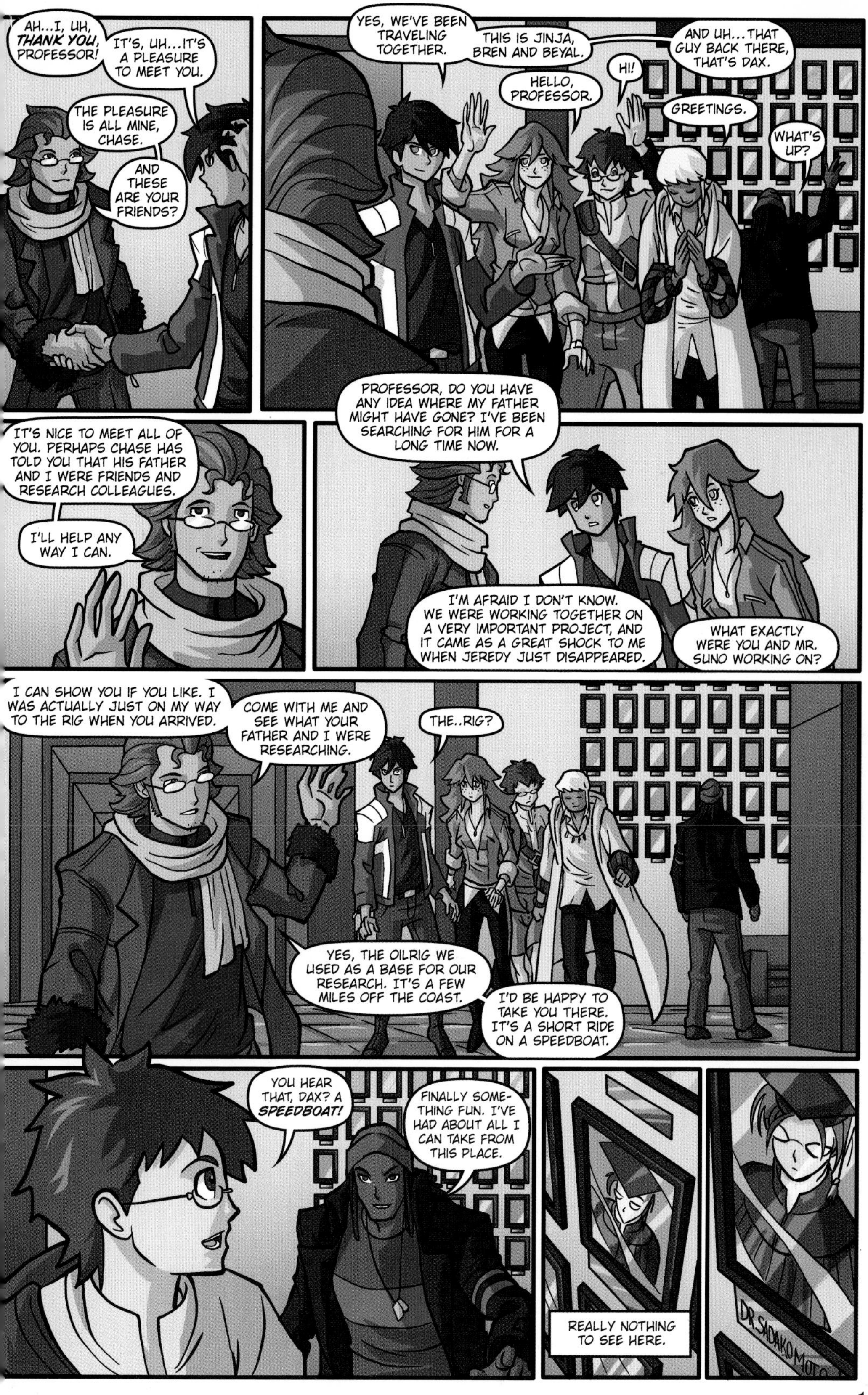

AH...I, UH, THANK YOU, PROFESSOR!
IT'S, UH...IT'S A PLEASURE TO MEET YOU.
THE PLEASURE IS ALL MINE, CHASE.
AND THESE ARE YOUR FRIENDS?
YES, WE'VE BEEN TRAVELING TOGETHER.
THIS IS JINJA, BREN AND BEYAL.
AND UH...THAT GUY BACK THERE, THAT'S DAX.
HELLO, PROFESSOR.
HI!
GREETINGS.
WHAT'S UP?
IT'S NICE TO MEET ALL OF YOU. PERHAPS CHASE HAS TOLD YOU THAT HIS FATHER AND I WERE FRIENDS AND RESEARCH COLLEAGUES.
I'LL HELP ANY WAY I CAN.
PROFESSOR, DO YOU HAVE ANY IDEA WHERE MY FATHER MIGHT HAVE GONE? I'VE BEEN SEARCHING FOR HIM FOR A LONG TIME NOW.
I'M AFRAID I DON'T KNOW. WE WERE WORKING TOGETHER ON A VERY IMPORTANT PROJECT, AND IT CAME AS A GREAT SHOCK TO ME WHEN JEREDY JUST DISAPPEARED.
WHAT EXACTLY WERE YOU AND MR. SUNO WORKING ON?
I CAN SHOW YOU IF YOU LIKE. I WAS ACTUALLY JUST ON MY WAY TO THE RIG WHEN YOU ARRIVED.
COME WITH ME AND SEE WHAT YOUR FATHER AND I WERE RESEARCHING.
THE..RIG?
YES, THE OILRIG WE USED AS A BASE FOR OUR RESEARCH. IT'S A FEW MILES OFF THE COAST.
I'D BE HAPPY TO TAKE YOU THERE. IT'S A SHORT RIDE ON A SPEEDBOAT.
YOU HEAR THAT, DAX? A SPEEDBOAT!
FINALLY SOMETHING FUN. I'VE HAD ABOUT ALL I CAN TAKE FROM THIS PLACE.
REALLY NOTHING TO SEE HERE.
DR. SADAKOMOTO

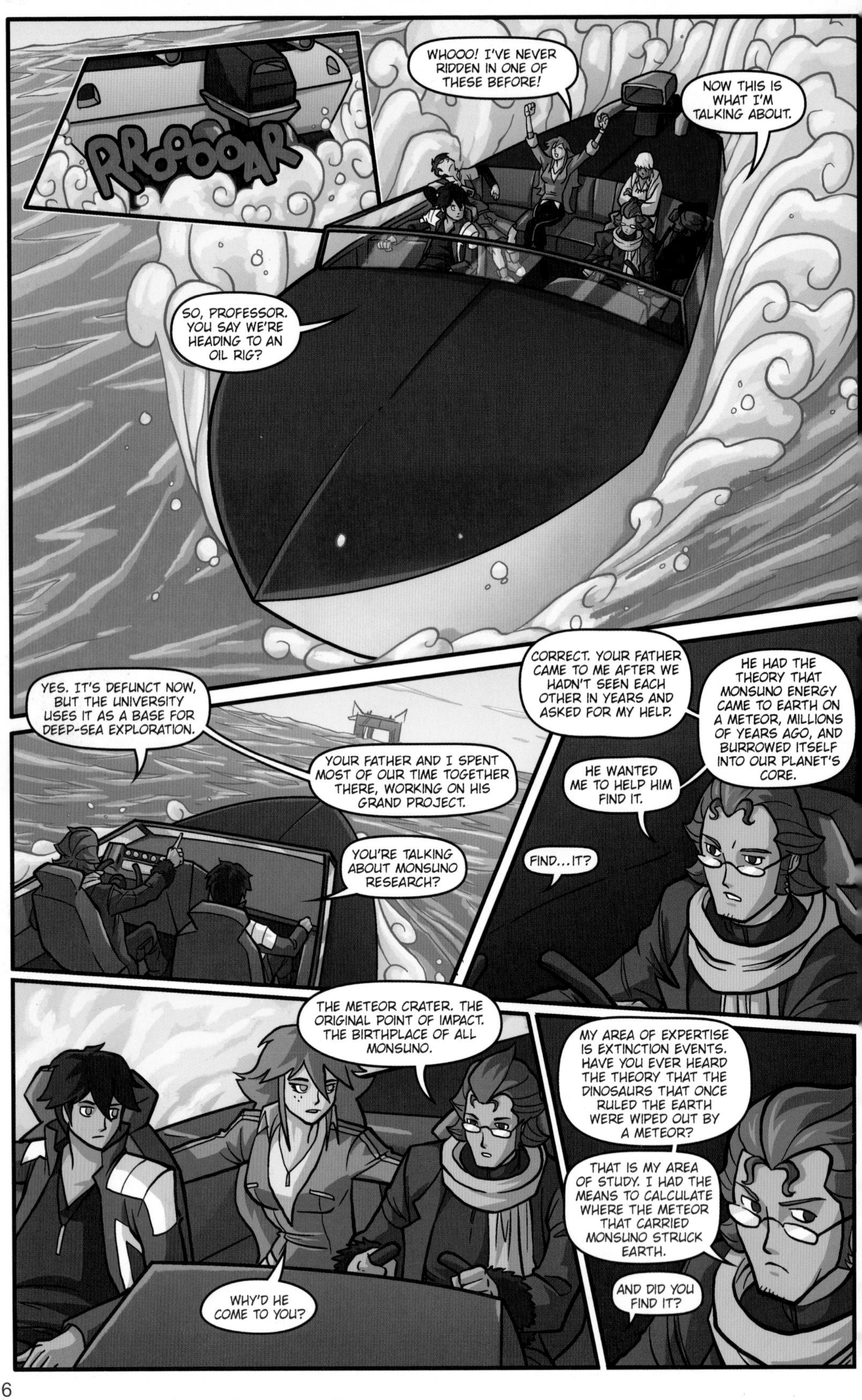
RROOOOAR
WHOOO! I'VE NEVER RIDDEN IN ONE OF THESE BEFORE!
NOW THIS IS WHAT I'M TALKING ABOUT.
SO, PROFESSOR. YOU SAY WE'RE HEADING TO AN OIL RIG?
YES. IT'S DEFUNCT NOW, BUT THE UNIVERSITY USES IT AS A BASE FOR DEEP-SEA EXPLORATION.
YOUR FATHER AND I SPENT MOST OF OUR TIME TOGETHER THERE, WORKING ON HIS GRAND PROJECT.
YOU'RE TALKING ABOUT MONSUNO RESEARCH?
CORRECT. YOUR FATHER CAME TO ME AFTER WE HADN'T SEEN EACH OTHER IN YEARS AND ASKED FOR MY HELP.
HE HAD THE THEORY THAT MONSUNO ENERGY CAME TO EARTH ON A METEOR, MILLIONS OF YEARS AGO, AND BURROWED ITSELF INTO OUR PLANET'S CORE.
HE WANTED ME TO HELP HIM FIND IT.
FIND...IT?
THE METEOR CRATER. THE ORIGINAL POINT OF IMPACT. THE BIRTHPLACE OF ALL MONSUNO.
WHY'D HE COME TO YOU?
MY AREA OF EXPERTISE IS EXTINCTION EVENTS. HAVE YOU EVER HEARD THE THEORY THAT THE DINOSAURS THAT ONCE RULED THE EARTH WERE WIPED OUT BY A METEOR?
THAT IS MY AREA OF STUDY. I HAD THE MEANS TO CALCULATE WHERE THE METEOR THAT CARRIED MONSUNO STRUCK EARTH.
AND DID YOU FIND IT?

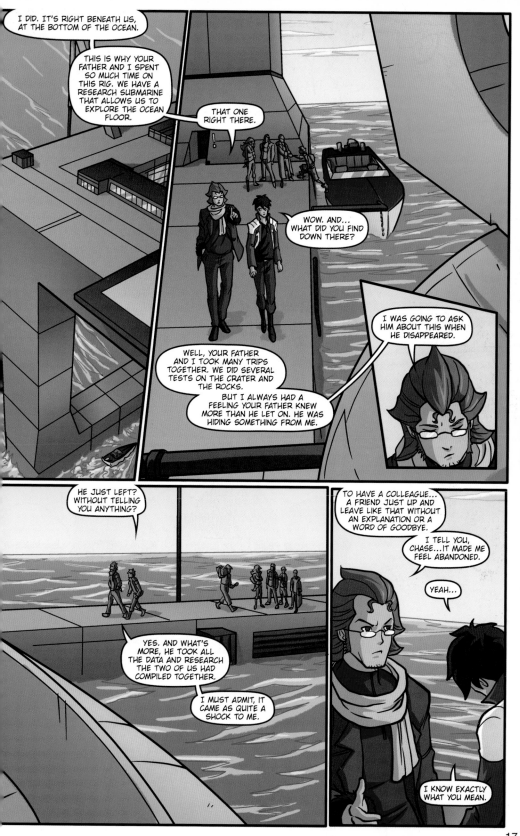

I DID. IT'S RIGHT BENEATH US, AT THE BOTTOM OF THE OCEAN.

THIS IS WHY YOUR FATHER AND I SPENT SO MUCH TIME ON THIS RIG. WE HAVE A RESEARCH SUBMARINE THAT ALLOWS US TO EXPLORE THE OCEAN FLOOR.

THAT ONE RIGHT THERE.

WOW. AND... WHAT DID YOU FIND DOWN THERE?

I WAS GOING TO ASK HIM ABOUT THIS WHEN HE DISAPPEARED.

WELL, YOUR FATHER AND I TOOK MANY TRIPS TOGETHER. WE DID SEVERAL TESTS ON THE CRATER AND THE ROCKS.

BUT I ALWAYS HAD A FEELING YOUR FATHER KNEW MORE THAN HE LET ON. HE WAS HIDING SOMETHING FROM ME.

HE JUST LEFT? WITHOUT TELLING YOU ANYTHING?

YES. AND WHAT'S MORE, HE TOOK ALL THE DATA AND RESEARCH THE TWO OF US HAD COMPILED TOGETHER.

I MUST ADMIT, IT CAME AS QUITE A SHOCK TO ME.

TO HAVE A COLLEAGUE... A FRIEND JUST UP AND LEAVE LIKE THAT WITHOUT AN EXPLANATION OR A WORD OF GOODBYE.

I TELL YOU, CHASE...IT MADE ME FEEL ABANDONED.

YEAH...

I KNOW EXACTLY WHAT YOU MEAN.

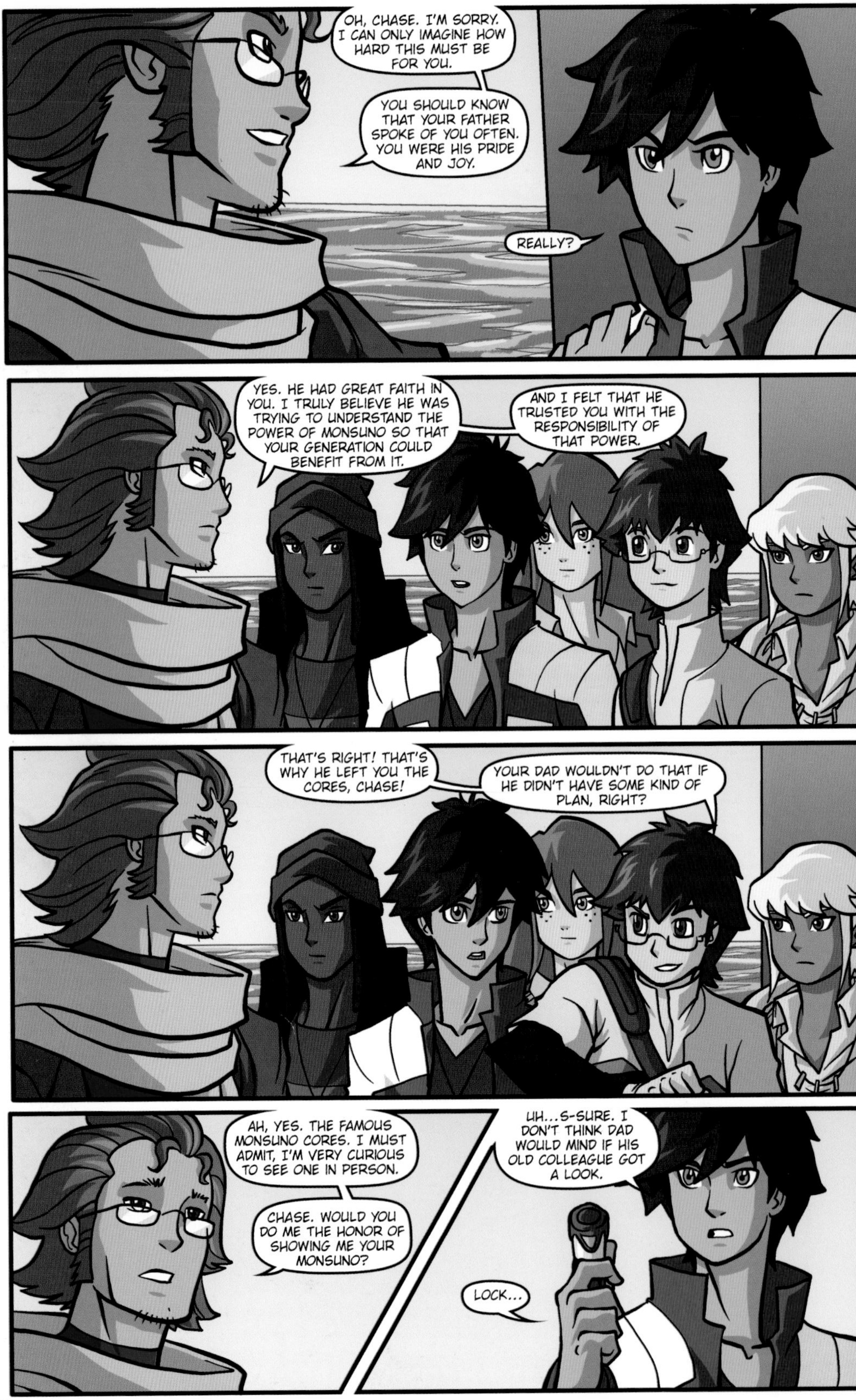
OH, CHASE. I'M SORRY. I CAN ONLY IMAGINE HOW HARD THIS MUST BE FOR YOU.
YOU SHOULD KNOW THAT YOUR FATHER SPOKE OF YOU OFTEN. YOU WERE HIS PRIDE AND JOY.
REALLY?
YES. HE HAD GREAT FAITH IN YOU. I TRULY BELIEVE HE WAS TRYING TO UNDERSTAND THE POWER OF MONSUNO SO THAT YOUR GENERATION COULD BENEFIT FROM IT.
AND I FELT THAT HE TRUSTED YOU WITH THE RESPONSIBILITY OF THAT POWER.
THAT'S RIGHT! THAT'S WHY HE LEFT YOU THE CORES, CHASE!
YOUR DAD WOULDN'T DO THAT IF HE DIDN'T HAVE SOME KIND OF PLAN, RIGHT?
AH, YES. THE FAMOUS MONSUNO CORES. I MUST ADMIT, I'M VERY CURIOUS TO SEE ONE IN PERSON.
CHASE. WOULD YOU DO ME THE HONOR OF SHOWING ME YOUR MONSUNO?
UH...S-SURE. I DON'T THINK DAD WOULD MIND IF HIS OLD COLLEAGUE GOT A LOOK.
LOCK...

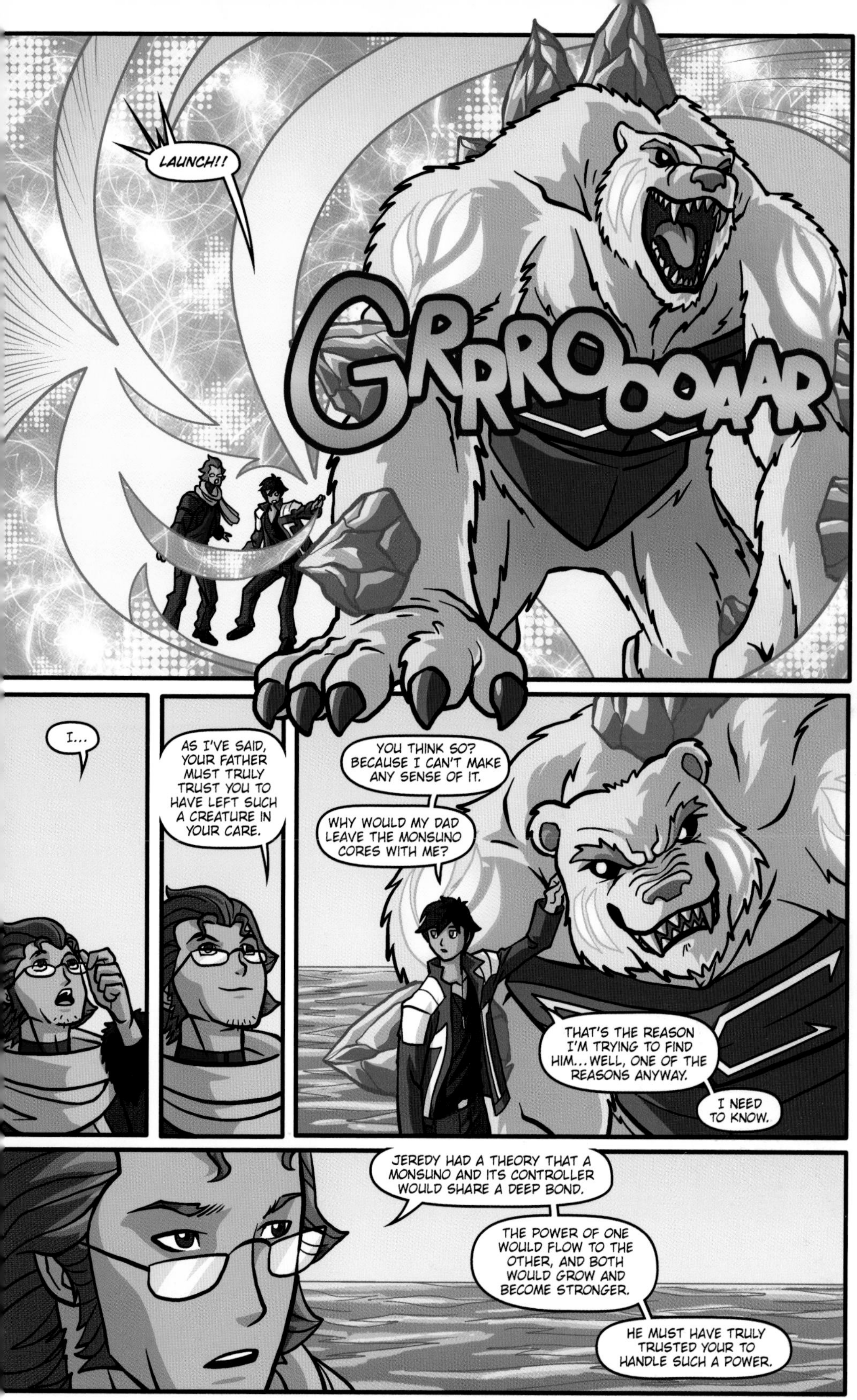
LAUNCH!!
GRRROOOOAAR
I...
AS I'VE SAID, YOUR FATHER MUST TRULY TRUST YOU TO HAVE LEFT SUCH A CREATURE IN YOUR CARE.
YOU THINK SO? BECAUSE I CAN'T MAKE ANY SENSE OF IT.
WHY WOULD MY DAD LEAVE THE MONSUNO CORES WITH ME?
THAT'S THE REASON I'M TRYING TO FIND HIM...WELL, ONE OF THE REASONS ANYWAY.
I NEED TO KNOW.
JEREDY HAD A THEORY THAT A MONSUNO AND ITS CONTROLLER WOULD SHARE A DEEP BOND.
THE POWER OF ONE WOULD FLOW TO THE OTHER, AND BOTH WOULD GROW AND BECOME STRONGER.
HE MUST HAVE TRULY TRUSTED YOUR TO HANDLE SUCH A POWER.

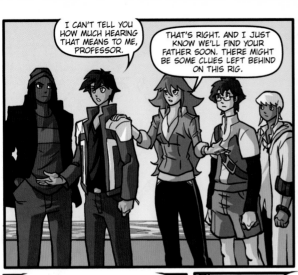

I CAN'T TELL YOU HOW MUCH HEARING THAT MEANS TO ME, PROFESSOR.

THAT'S RIGHT. AND I JUST KNOW WE'LL FIND YOUR FATHER SOON. THERE MIGHT BE SOME CLUES LEFT BEHIND ON THIS RIG.

YOU ARE MORE THAN WELCOME TO HAVE A LOOK AROUND. THE CREW HAS BEEN INFORMED AND WILL NOT BOTHER YOU.

BUT, CHASE, I WONDER IF I MIGHT ASK YOU FOR A...FAVOR.

I'M SCHEDULED TO TAKE ANOTHER DIVE TODAY, AND I WAS HOPING YOU AND LOCK COULD JOIN ME.

UH...ARE YOU SURE THAT'S OKAY? WILL HE EVEN FIT?

OH YES, THE SUB-MARINE'S INTERIOR IS QUITE LARGE.

AND I THINK IT WOULD MAKE YOUR FATHER PROUD TO HAVE HIS SON AND HIS MONSUNO THERE WHEN WE FOLLOW IN HIS FOOTSTEPS.

WELL...

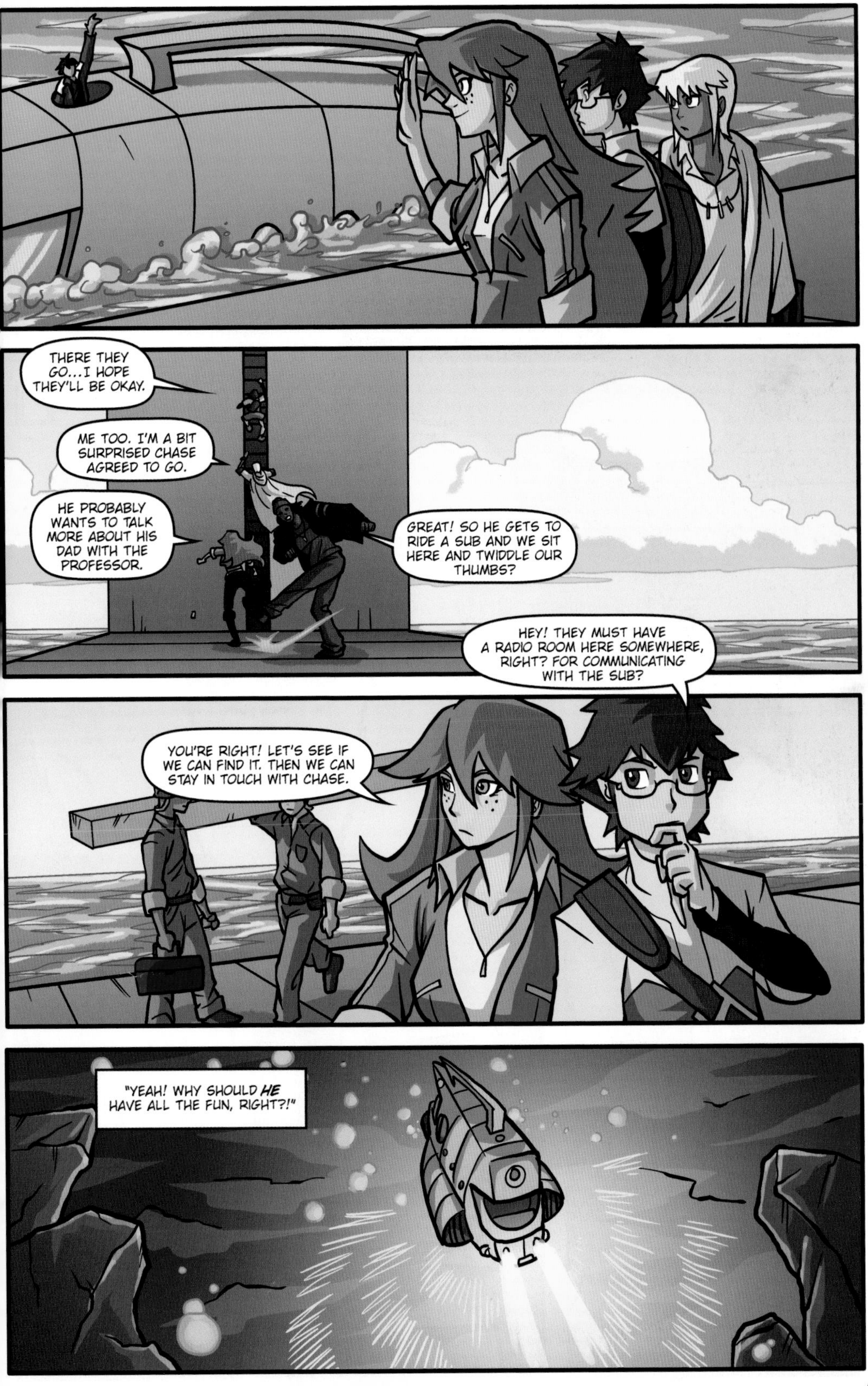
THERE THEY GO...I HOPE THEY'LL BE OKAY.
ME TOO. I'M A BIT SURPRISED CHASE AGREED TO GO.
HE PROBABLY WANTS TO TALK MORE ABOUT HIS DAD WITH THE PROFESSOR.
GREAT! SO HE GETS TO RIDE A SUB AND WE SIT HERE AND TWIDDLE OUR THUMBS?
HEY! THEY MUST HAVE A RADIO ROOM HERE SOMEWHERE, RIGHT? FOR COMMUNICATING WITH THE SUB?
YOU'RE RIGHT! LET'S SEE IF WE CAN FIND IT. THEN WE CAN STAY IN TOUCH WITH CHASE.
"YEAH! WHY SHOULD ***HE*** HAVE ALL THE FUN, RIGHT?!"

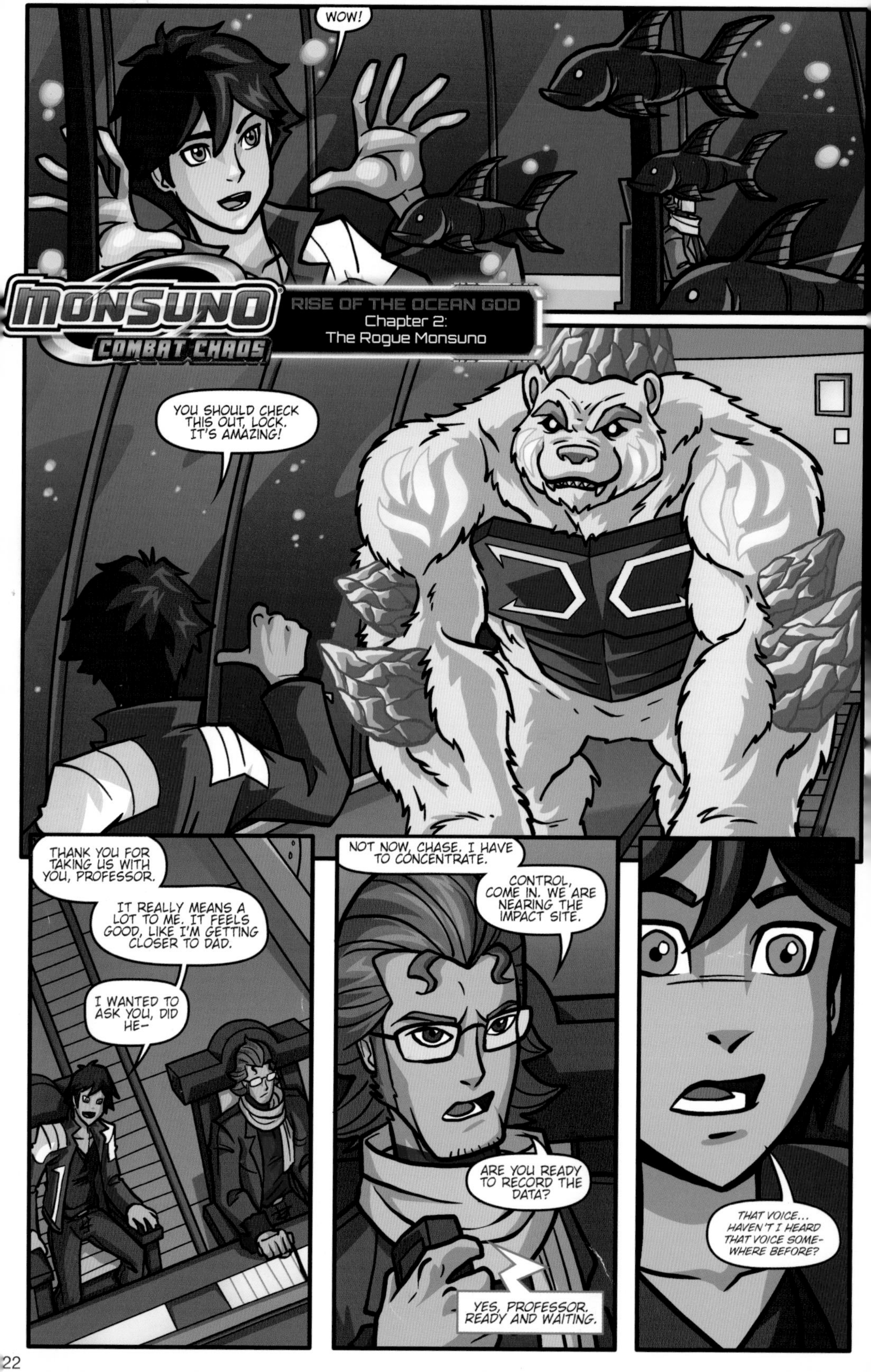
WOW!
MONSUNO COMBAT CHAOS
RISE OF THE OCEAN GOD
Chapter 2:
The Rogue Monsuno
YOU SHOULD CHECK THIS OUT, LOCK. IT'S AMAZING!
THANK YOU FOR TAKING US WITH YOU, PROFESSOR.
IT REALLY MEANS A LOT TO ME. IT FEELS GOOD, LIKE I'M GETTING CLOSER TO DAD.
I WANTED TO ASK YOU, DID HE–
NOT NOW, CHASE. I HAVE TO CONCENTRATE.
CONTROL, COME IN. WE ARE NEARING THE IMPACT SITE.
ARE YOU READY TO RECORD THE DATA?
YES, PROFESSOR. READY AND WAITING.
THAT VOICE... HAVEN'T I HEARD THAT VOICE SOME-WHERE BEFORE?

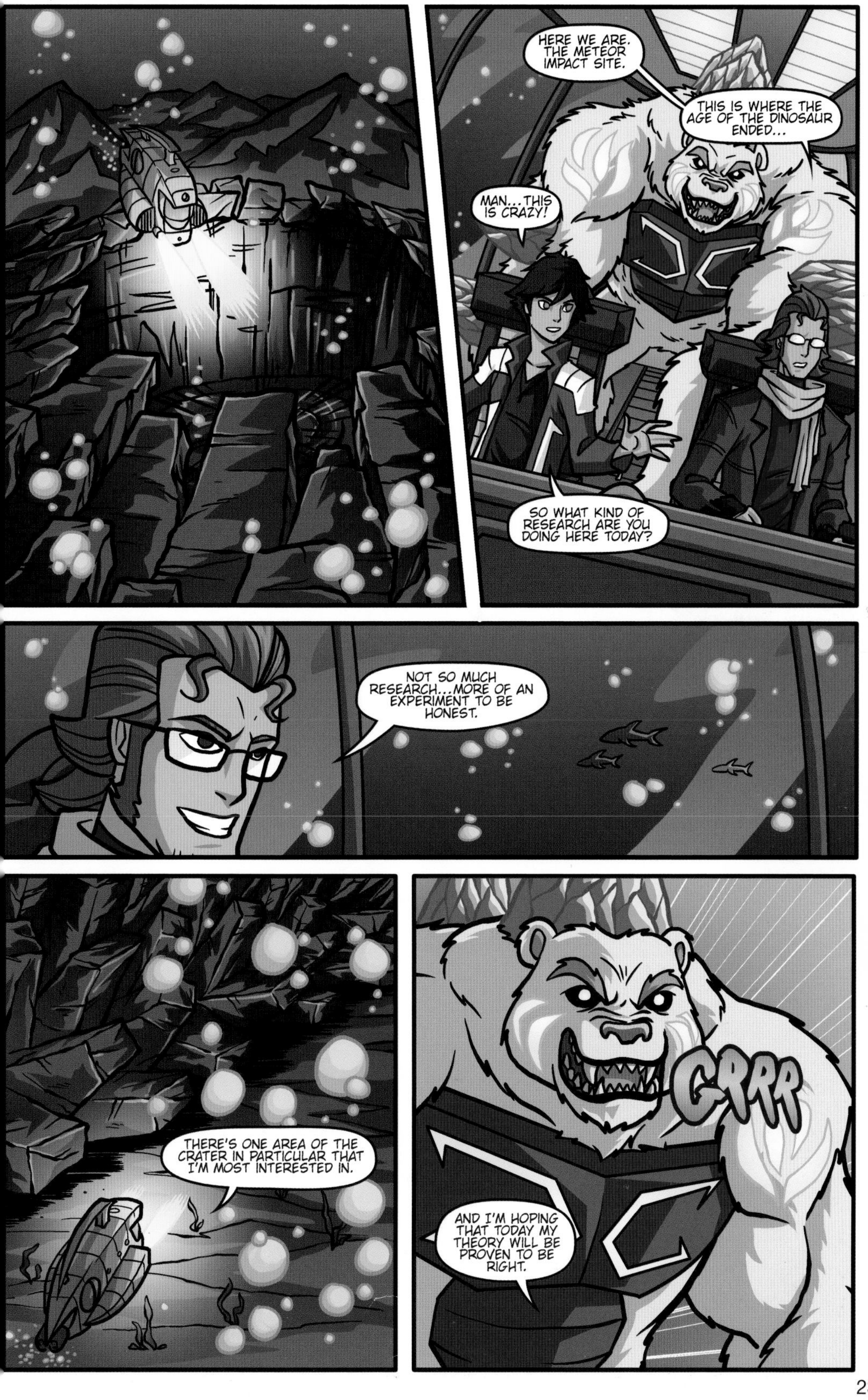
HERE WE ARE. THE METEOR IMPACT SITE.
THIS IS WHERE THE AGE OF THE DINOSAUR ENDED...
MAN...THIS IS CRAZY!
SO WHAT KIND OF RESEARCH ARE YOU DOING HERE TODAY?
NOT SO MUCH RESEARCH...MORE OF AN EXPERIMENT TO BE HONEST.
THERE'S ONE AREA OF THE CRATER IN PARTICULAR THAT I'M MOST INTERESTED IN.
GRRR
AND I'M HOPING THAT TODAY MY THEORY WILL BE PROVEN TO BE RIGHT.

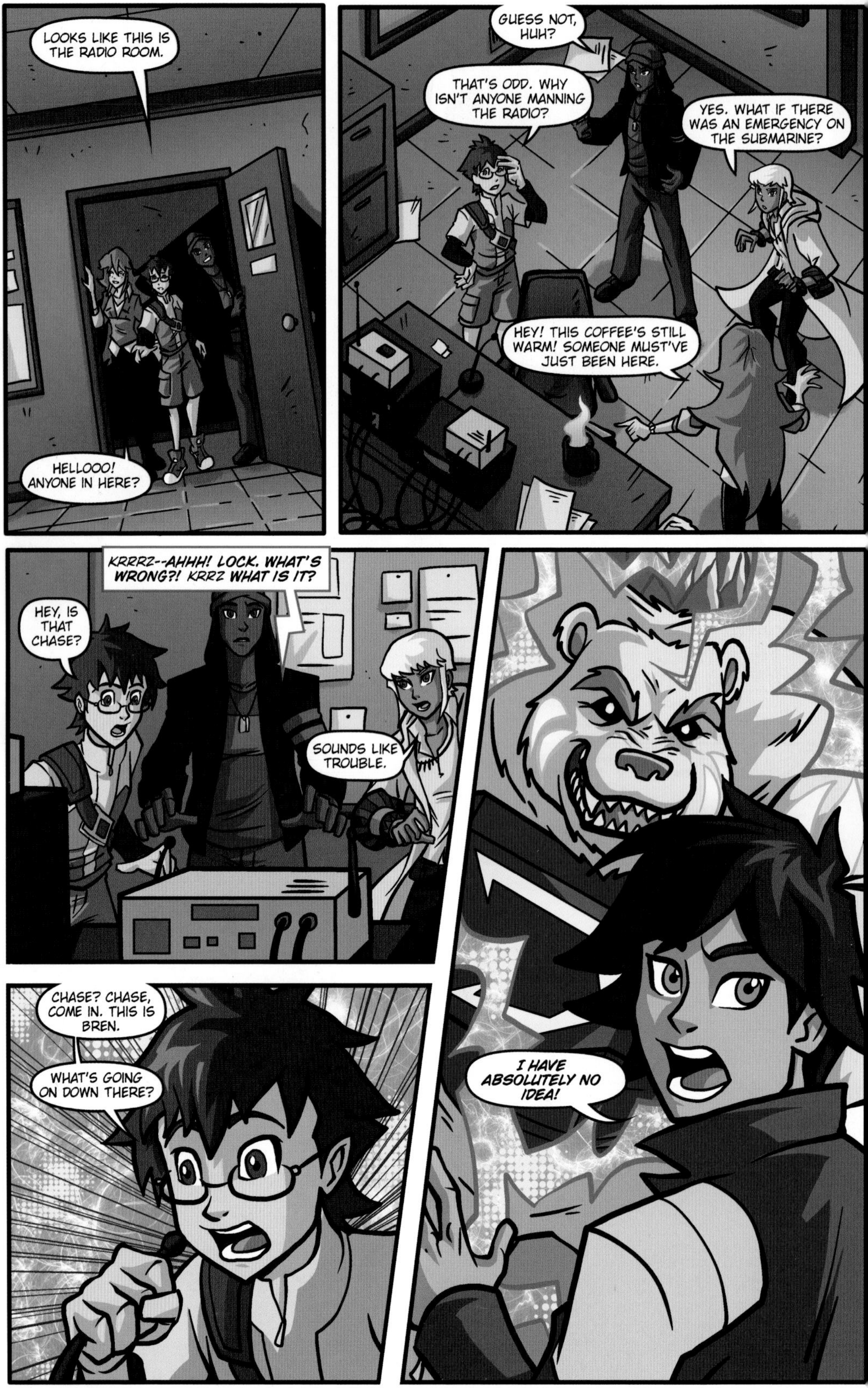
LOOKS LIKE THIS IS THE RADIO ROOM.
HELLOOO! ANYONE IN HERE?
GUESS NOT, HUH?
THAT'S ODD. WHY ISN'T ANYONE MANNING THE RADIO?
YES. WHAT IF THERE WAS AN EMERGENCY ON THE SUBMARINE?
HEY! THIS COFFEE'S STILL WARM! SOMEONE MUST'VE JUST BEEN HERE.
KRRRZ--AHHH! LOCK. WHAT'S WRONG?! KRRZ WHAT IS IT?
HEY, IS THAT CHASE?
SOUNDS LIKE TROUBLE.
I HAVE ABSOLUTELY NO IDEA!
CHASE? CHASE, COME IN. THIS IS BREN.
WHAT'S GOING ON DOWN THERE?

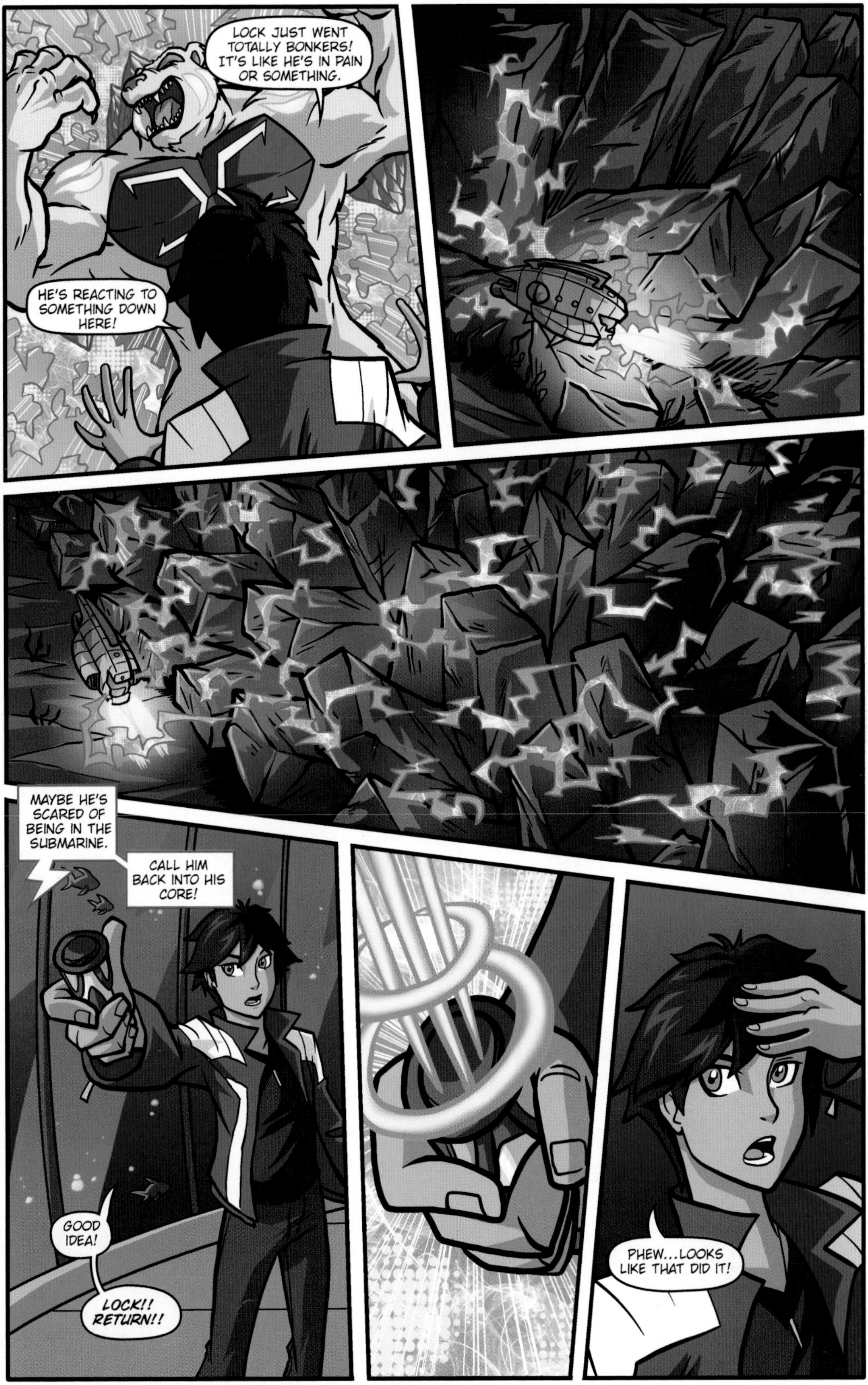
LOCK JUST WENT TOTALLY BONKERS! IT'S LIKE HE'S IN PAIN OR SOMETHING.
HE'S REACTING TO SOMETHING DOWN HERE!
MAYBE HE'S SCARED OF BEING IN THE SUBMARINE.
CALL HIM BACK INTO HIS CORE!
GOOD IDEA!
LOCK!! RETURN!!
PHEW...LOOKS LIKE THAT DID IT!

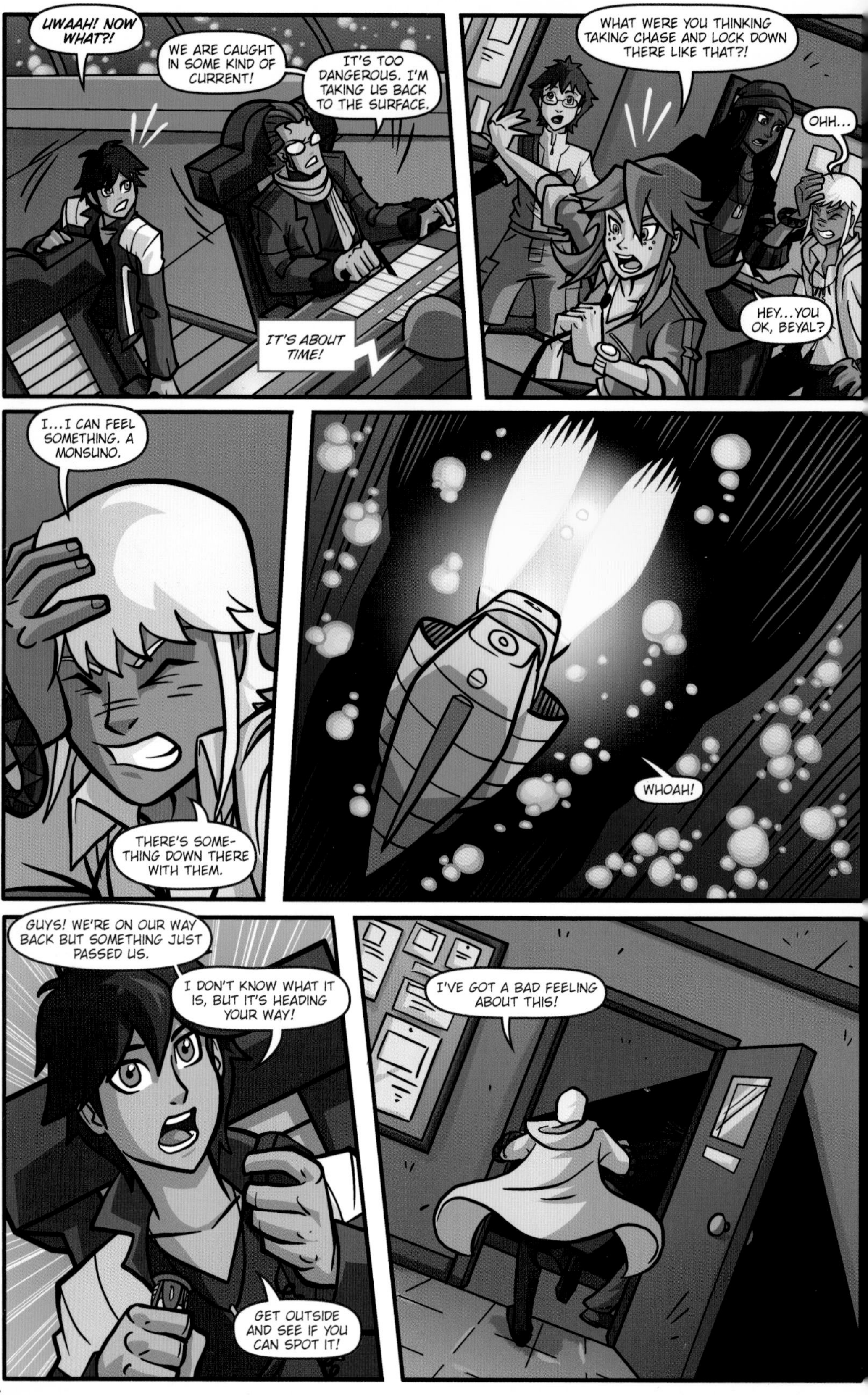
UWAAH! NOW WHAT?!
WE ARE CAUGHT IN SOME KIND OF CURRENT!
IT'S TOO DANGEROUS. I'M TAKING US BACK TO THE SURFACE.
IT'S ABOUT TIME!
WHAT WERE YOU THINKING TAKING CHASE AND LOCK DOWN THERE LIKE THAT?!
OHH...
HEY...YOU OK, BEYAL?
I...I CAN FEEL SOMETHING. A MONSUNO.
THERE'S SOME-THING DOWN THERE WITH THEM.
WHOAH!
GUYS! WE'RE ON OUR WAY BACK BUT SOMETHING JUST PASSED US.
I DON'T KNOW WHAT IT IS, BUT IT'S HEADING YOUR WAY!
GET OUTSIDE AND SEE IF YOU CAN SPOT IT!
I'VE GOT A BAD FEELING ABOUT THIS!

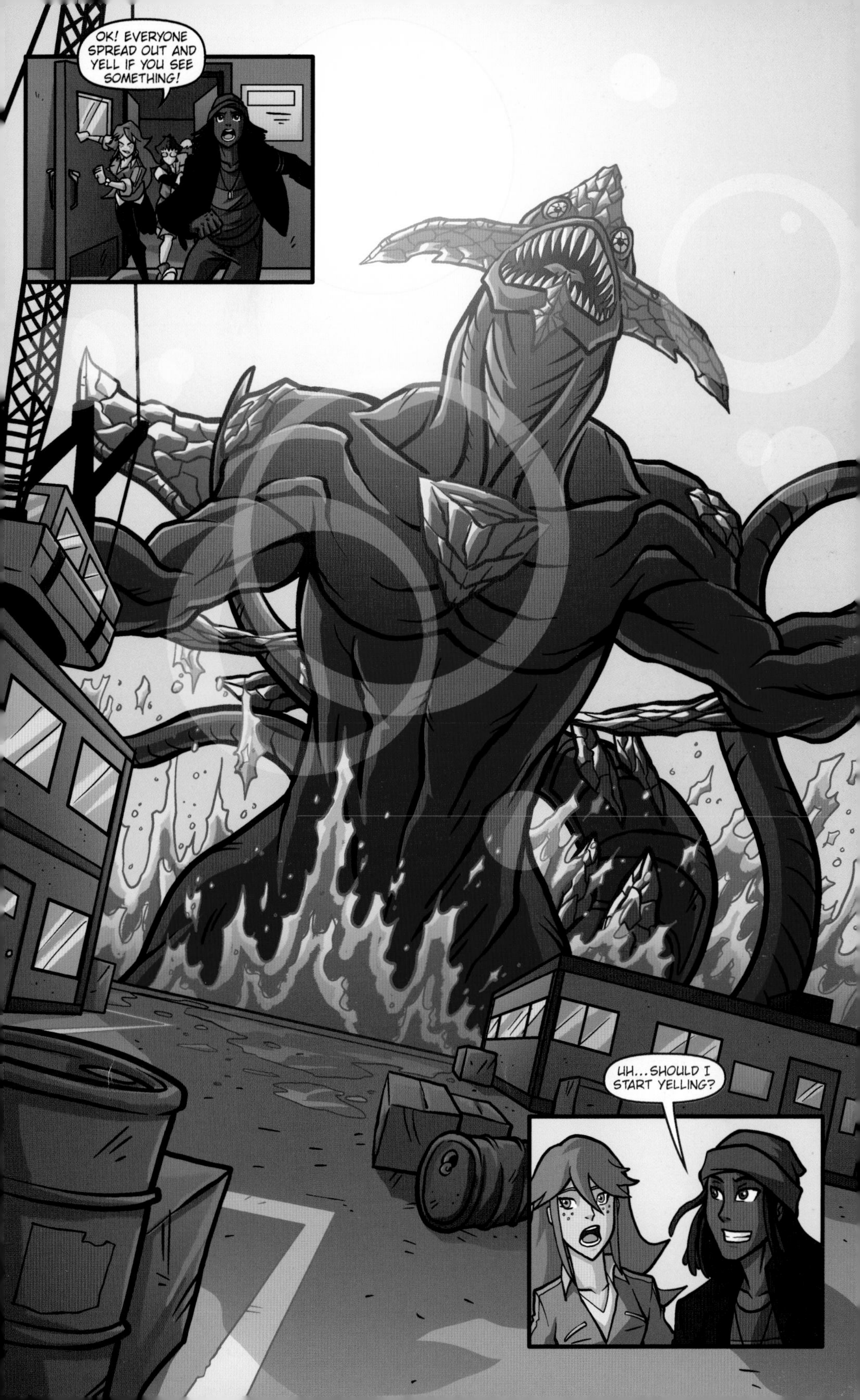
OK! EVERYONE SPREAD OUT AND YELL IF YOU SEE SOMETHING!
UH...SHOULD I START YELLING?

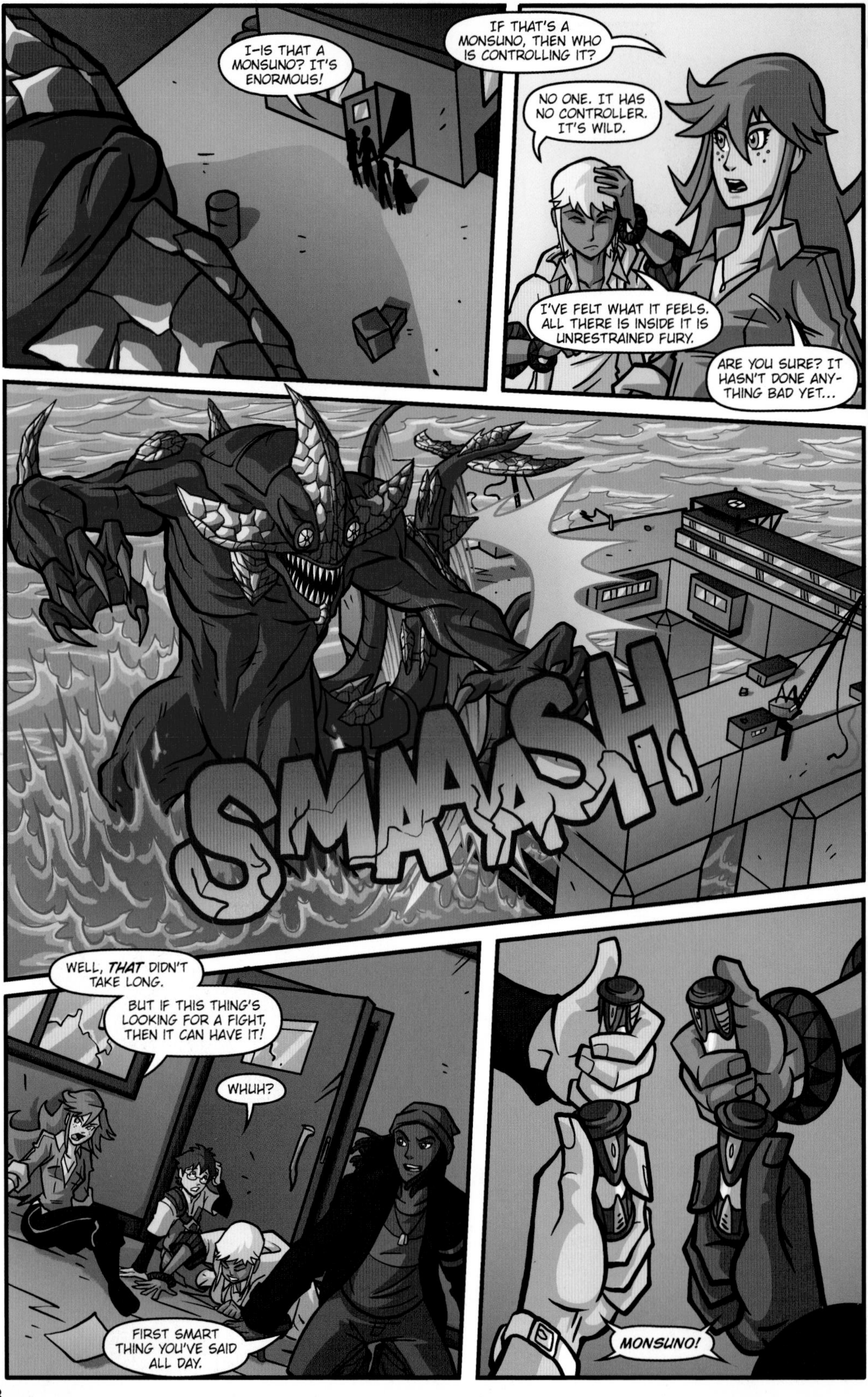
I–IS THAT A MONSUNO? IT'S ENORMOUS!
IF THAT'S A MONSUNO, THEN WHO IS CONTROLLING IT?
NO ONE. IT HAS NO CONTROLLER. IT'S WILD.
I'VE FELT WHAT IT FEELS. ALL THERE IS INSIDE IT IS UNRESTRAINED FURY.
ARE YOU SURE? IT HASN'T DONE ANYTHING BAD YET...
SMAASH!
WELL, *THAT* DIDN'T TAKE LONG.
BUT IF THIS THING'S LOOKING FOR A FIGHT, THEN IT CAN HAVE IT!
WHUH?
FIRST SMART THING YOU'VE SAID ALL DAY.
MONSUNO!

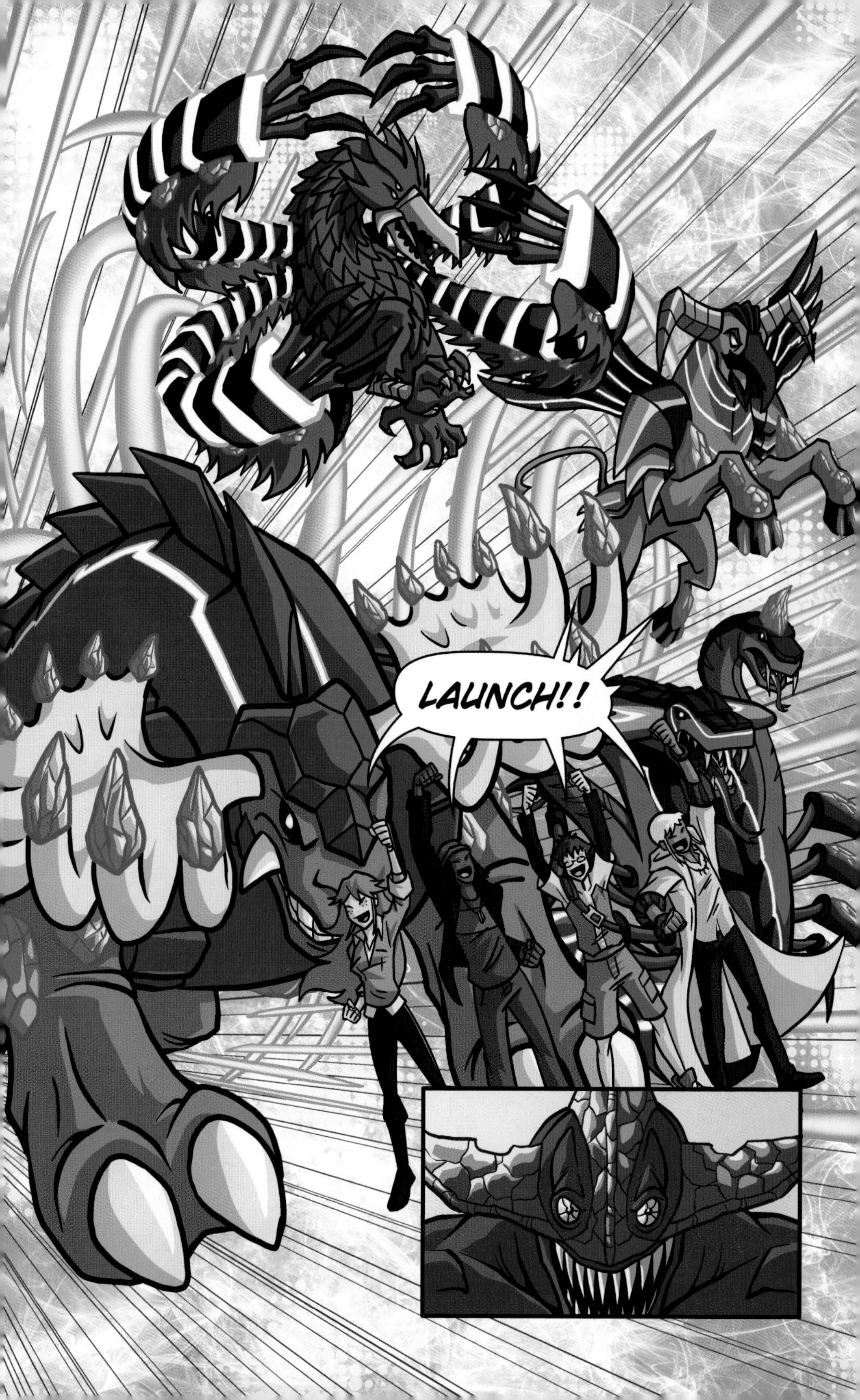
LAUNCH!!

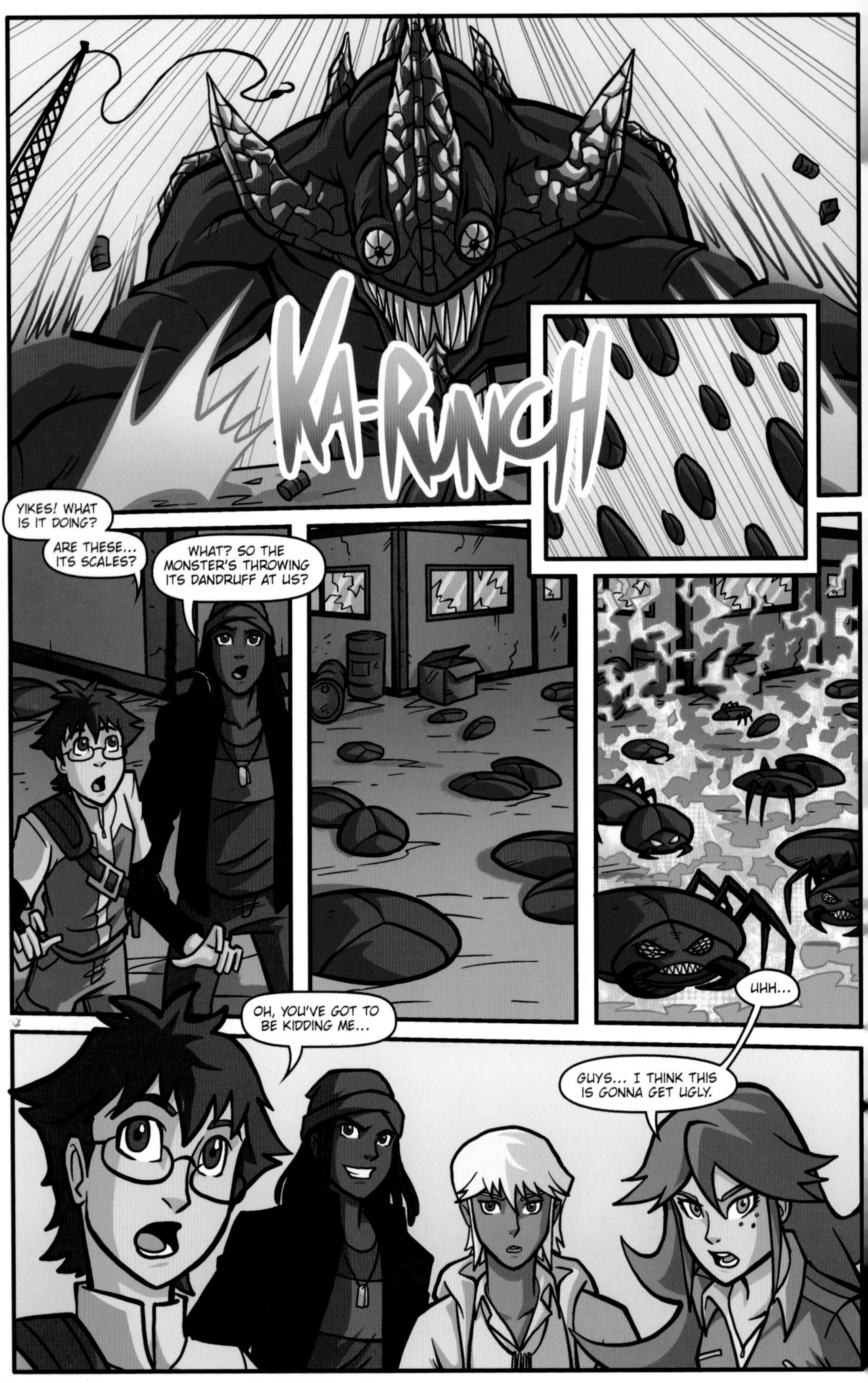
KA-RUNCH
YIKES! WHAT IS IT DOING?
ARE THESE... ITS SCALES?
WHAT? SO THE MONSTER'S THROWING ITS DANDRUFF AT US?
OH, YOU'VE GOT TO BE KIDDING ME...
UHH...
GUYS... I THINK THIS IS GONNA GET UGLY.

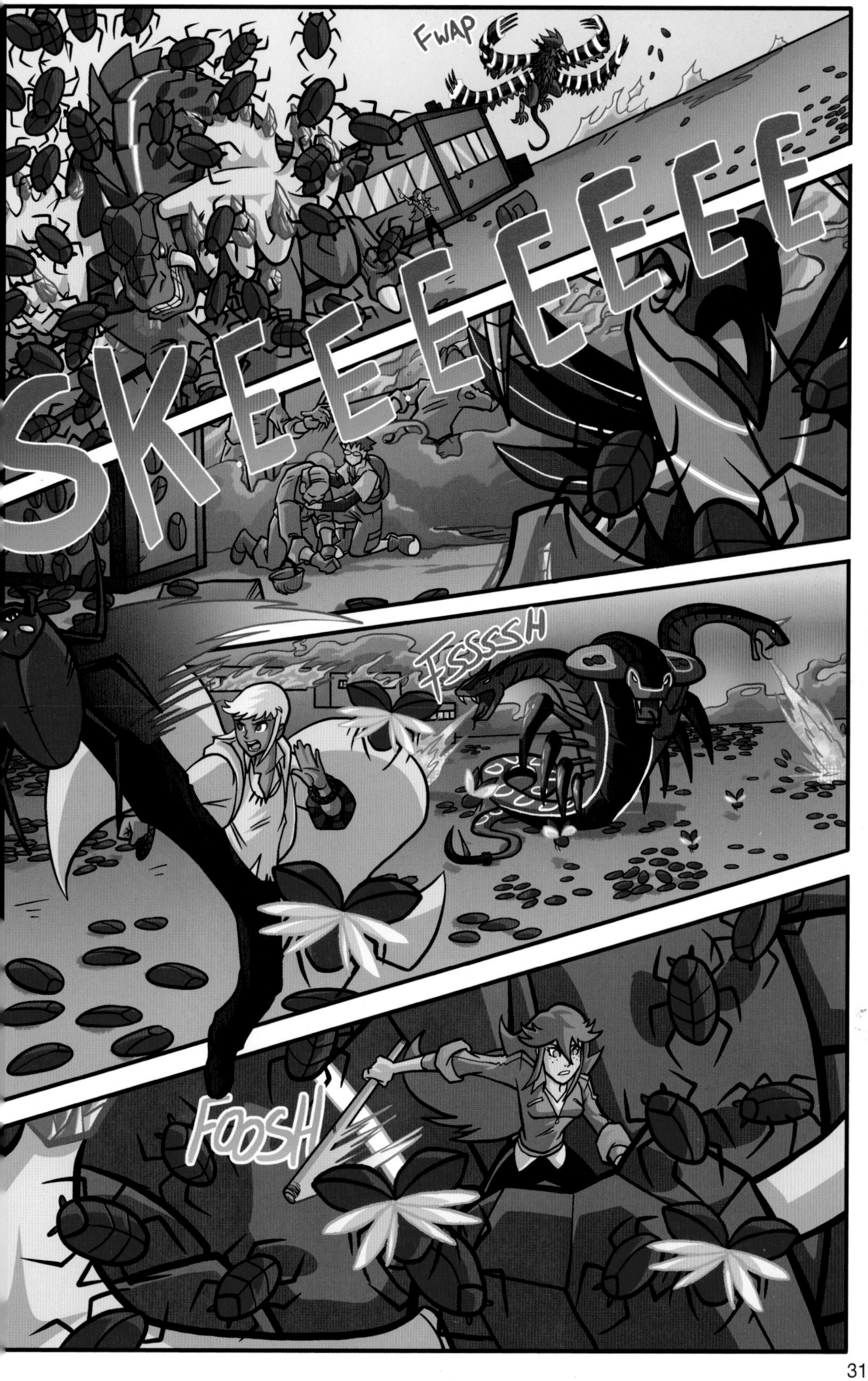
FWAP
SKEEEEEEEE
FSSSSH
FOOSH

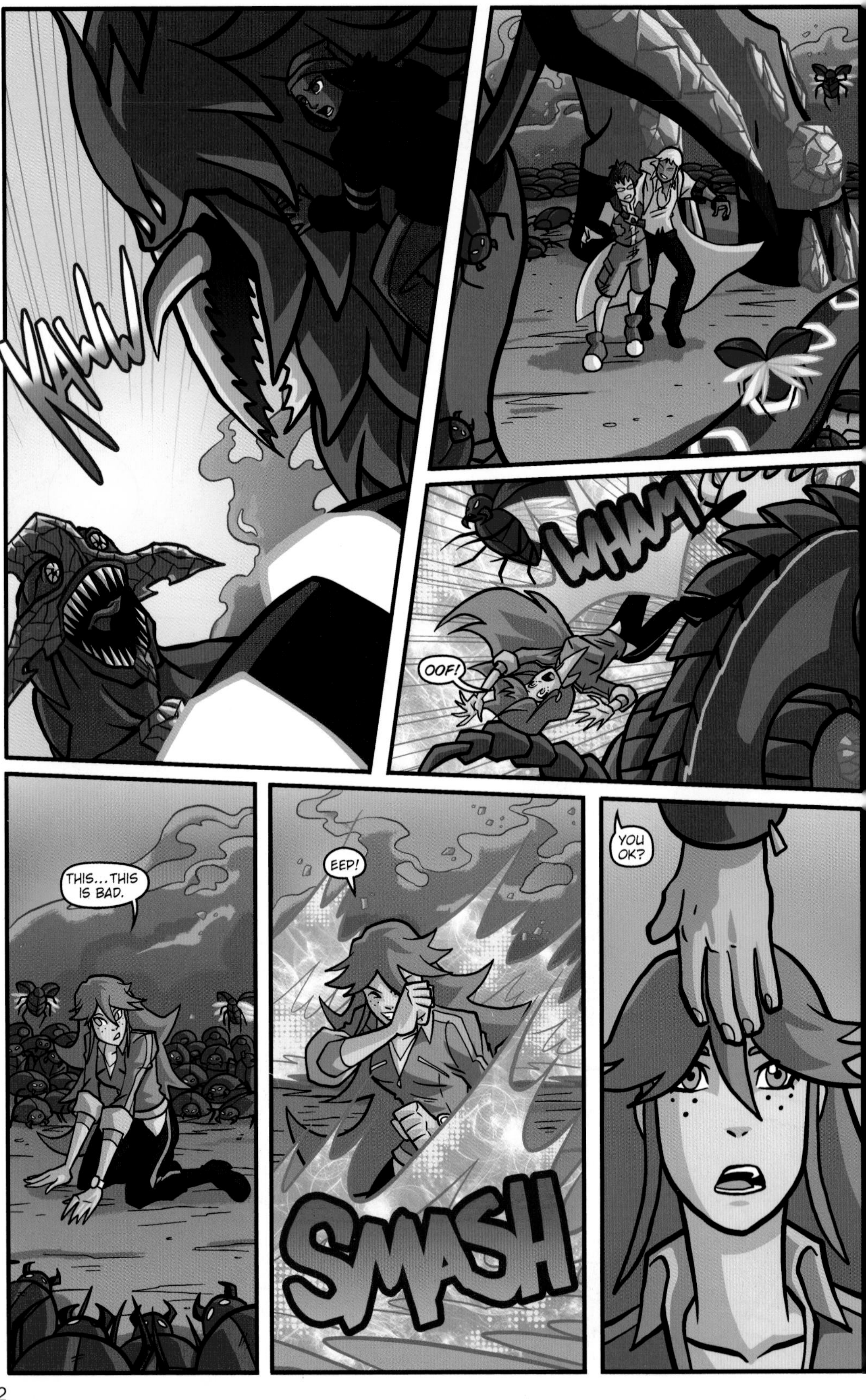
KAWW
WHAM
OOF!
THIS...THIS IS BAD.
EEP!
SMASH
YOU OK?

LOOKS LIKE WE MADE IT BACK JUST IN TIME.

NO KIDDING.

THANKS FOR THE RESCUE. IS THE PROFESSOR...

HE'S FINE. WE SPLIT UP TO LOOK FOR YOU.

SPEAKING OF WHICH, WHERE IS EVERYONE?!

YOU'RE BACK! DIDN'T WANT TO MISS ALL THE FUN, HUH?

HEH HEH... OUCH.

I'M GLAD TO SEE YOU'RE BOTH SAFE.

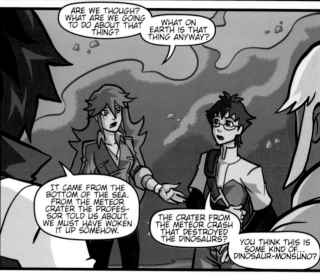

ARE WE THOUGH? WHAT ARE WE GOING TO DO ABOUT THAT THING?

WHAT ON EARTH IS THAT THING ANYWAY?

IT CAME FROM THE BOTTOM OF THE SEA. FROM THE METEOR CRATER THE PROFESSOR TOLD US ABOUT. WE MUST HAVE WOKEN IT UP SOMEHOW.

THE CRATER FROM THE METEOR CRASH THAT DESTROYED THE DINOSAURS?

YOU THINK THIS IS SOME KIND OF... DINOSAUR-MONSÛNO?

IT'S POSSIBLE, RIGHT? THAT MUST'VE BEEN WHAT MY DAD WAS SEARCHING...

HEY! WHERE'S DAX?

LOOK!

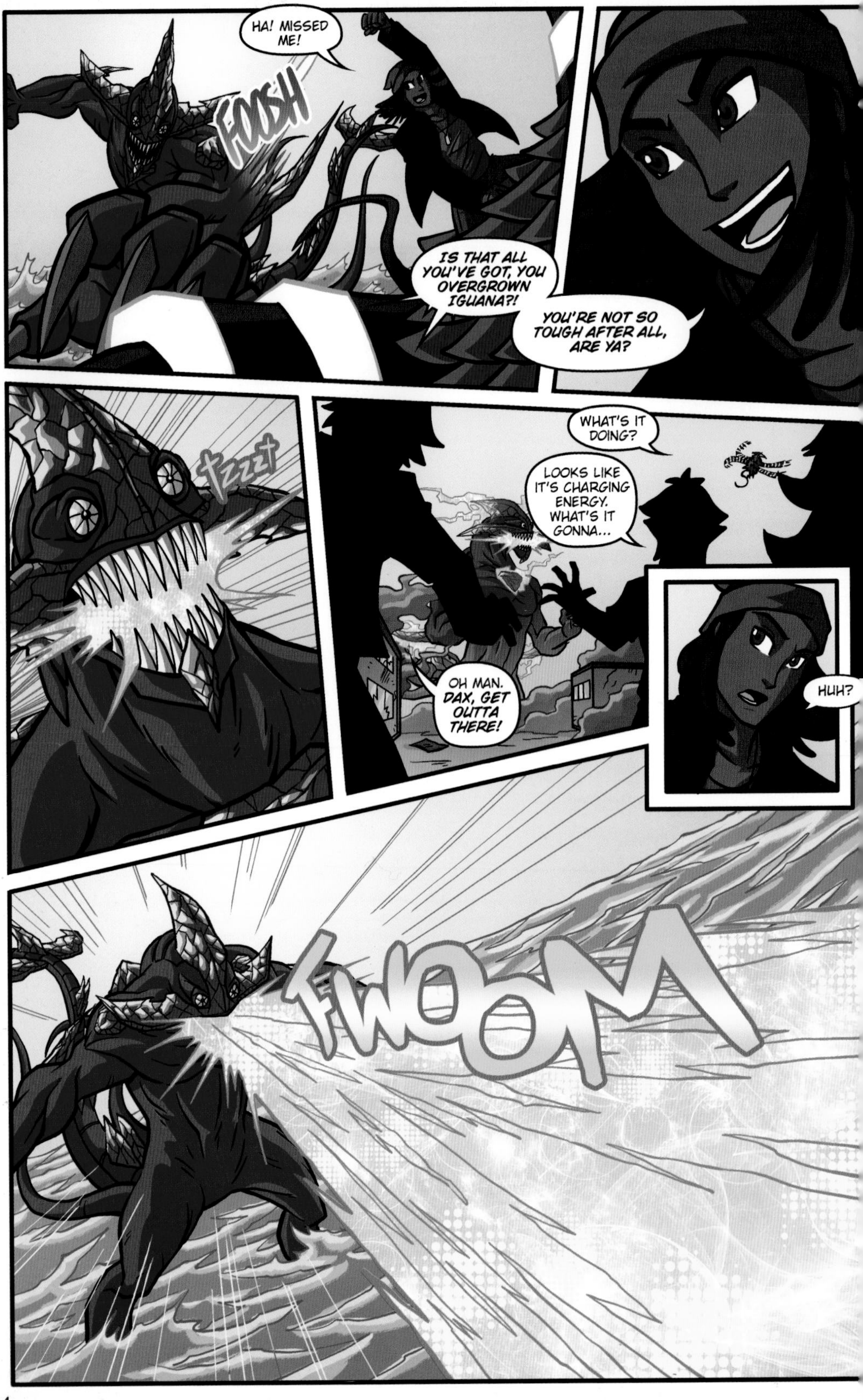
HA! MISSED ME!
FOOSH
IS THAT ALL YOU'VE GOT, YOU OVERGROWN IGUANA?!
YOU'RE NOT SO TOUGH AFTER ALL, ARE YA?
TZZZT
WHAT'S IT DOING?
LOOKS LIKE IT'S CHARGING ENERGY. WHAT'S IT GONNA...
OH MAN. DAX, GET OUTTA THERE!
HUH?
FWOOM

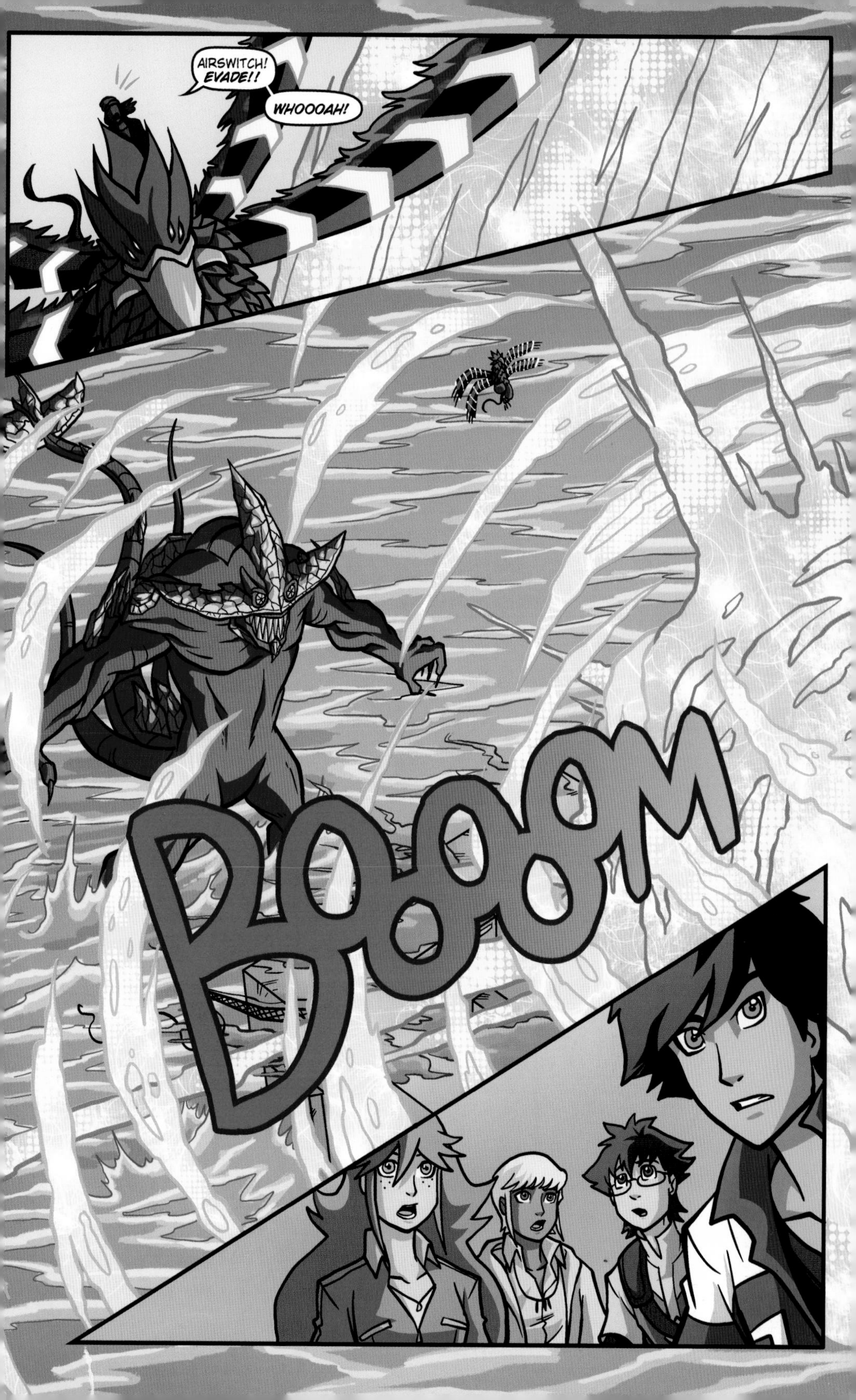
AIRSWITCH! EVADE!!
WHOOOAH!
BOOOOM

COMING IN FOR A LANDING!

HI GUYS...UH...I JUST ALMOST GOT *VAPORIZED!*

WE SAW! YOU'RE LUCKY TO BE ALIVE.

AIN'T IT THE TRUTH! WHY'D YOU GO AND MAKE IT MAD LIKE THAT?

WHAT *IS* THAT THING, ANYWAY?!

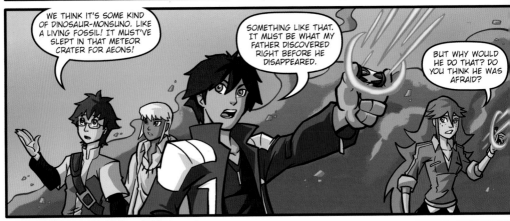

WE THINK IT'S SOME KIND OF DINOSAUR-MONSUNO. LIKE A LIVING FOSSIL! IT MUST'VE SLEPT IN THAT METEOR CRATER FOR AEONS!

SOMETHING LIKE THAT. IT MUST BE WHAT MY FATHER DISCOVERED RIGHT BEFORE HE DISAPPEARED.

BUT WHY WOULD HE DO THAT? DO YOU THINK HE WAS AFRAID?

I...I DON'T KNOW. MAYBE HE JUST DIDN'T WANT TO RISK WAKING IT. MAYBE HE KNEW WHAT IT WOULD DO.

WELL, IT'S *AWAKE NOW.* AND IT'S *HEADING FOR THE MAINLAND.*

ARE WE GONNA DO SOMETHING ABOUT IT OR WHAT?

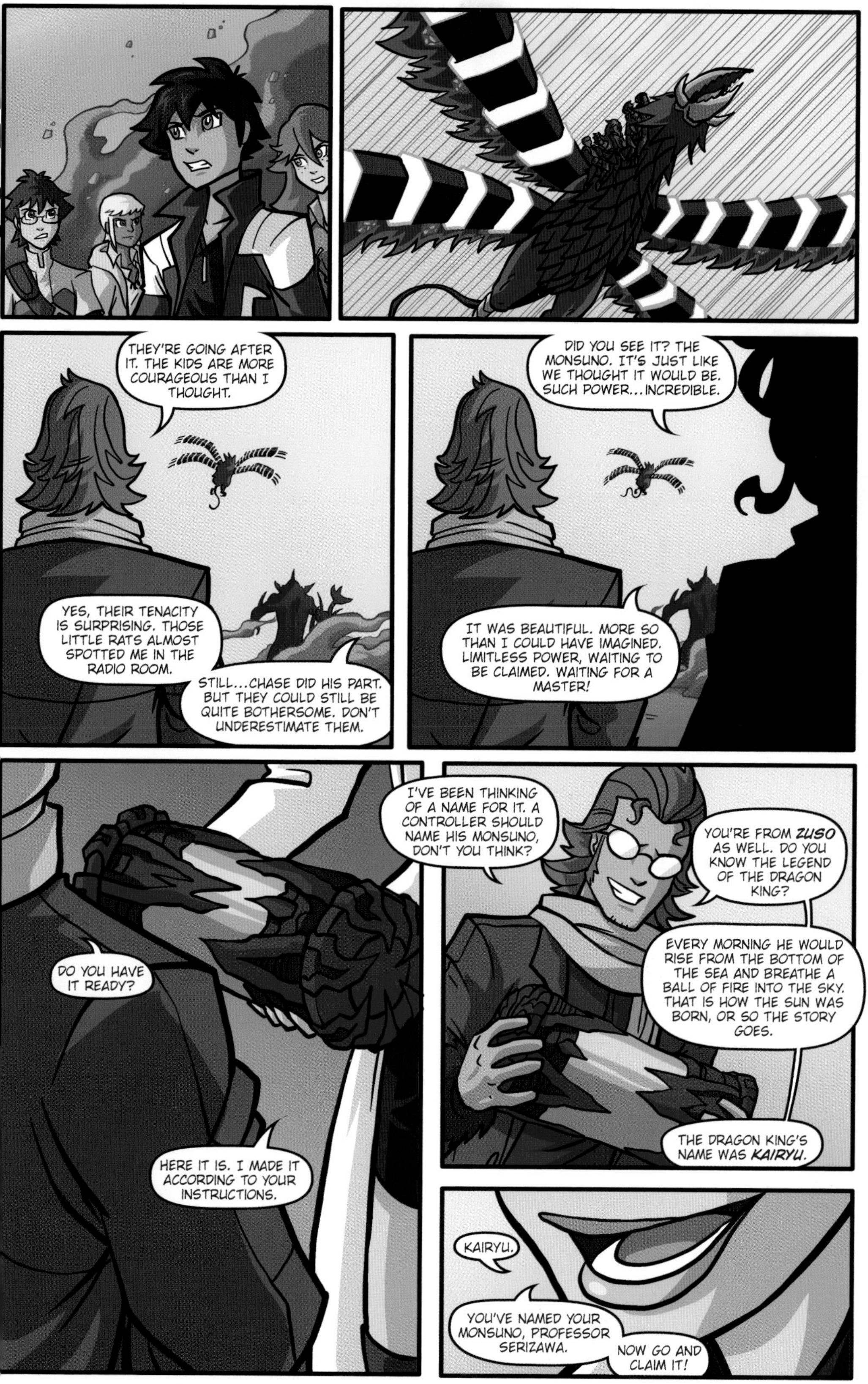
THEY'RE GOING AFTER IT. THE KIDS ARE MORE COURAGEOUS THAN I THOUGHT.
YES, THEIR TENACITY IS SURPRISING. THOSE LITTLE RATS ALMOST SPOTTED ME IN THE RADIO ROOM.
STILL...CHASE DID HIS PART. BUT THEY COULD STILL BE QUITE BOTHERSOME. DON'T UNDERESTIMATE THEM.
DID YOU SEE IT? THE MONSUNO. IT'S JUST LIKE WE THOUGHT IT WOULD BE. SUCH POWER...INCREDIBLE.
IT WAS BEAUTIFUL. MORE SO THAN I COULD HAVE IMAGINED. LIMITLESS POWER, WAITING TO BE CLAIMED. WAITING FOR A MASTER!
DO YOU HAVE IT READY?
HERE IT IS. I MADE IT ACCORDING TO YOUR INSTRUCTIONS.
I'VE BEEN THINKING OF A NAME FOR IT. A CONTROLLER SHOULD NAME HIS MONSUNO, DON'T YOU THINK?
YOU'RE FROM ZUSO AS WELL. DO YOU KNOW THE LEGEND OF THE DRAGON KING?
EVERY MORNING HE WOULD RISE FROM THE BOTTOM OF THE SEA AND BREATHE A BALL OF FIRE INTO THE SKY. THAT IS HOW THE SUN WAS BORN, OR SO THE STORY GOES.
THE DRAGON KING'S NAME WAS KAIRYU.
KAIRYU.
YOU'VE NAMED YOUR MONSUNO, PROFESSOR SERIZAWA.
NOW GO AND CLAIM IT!

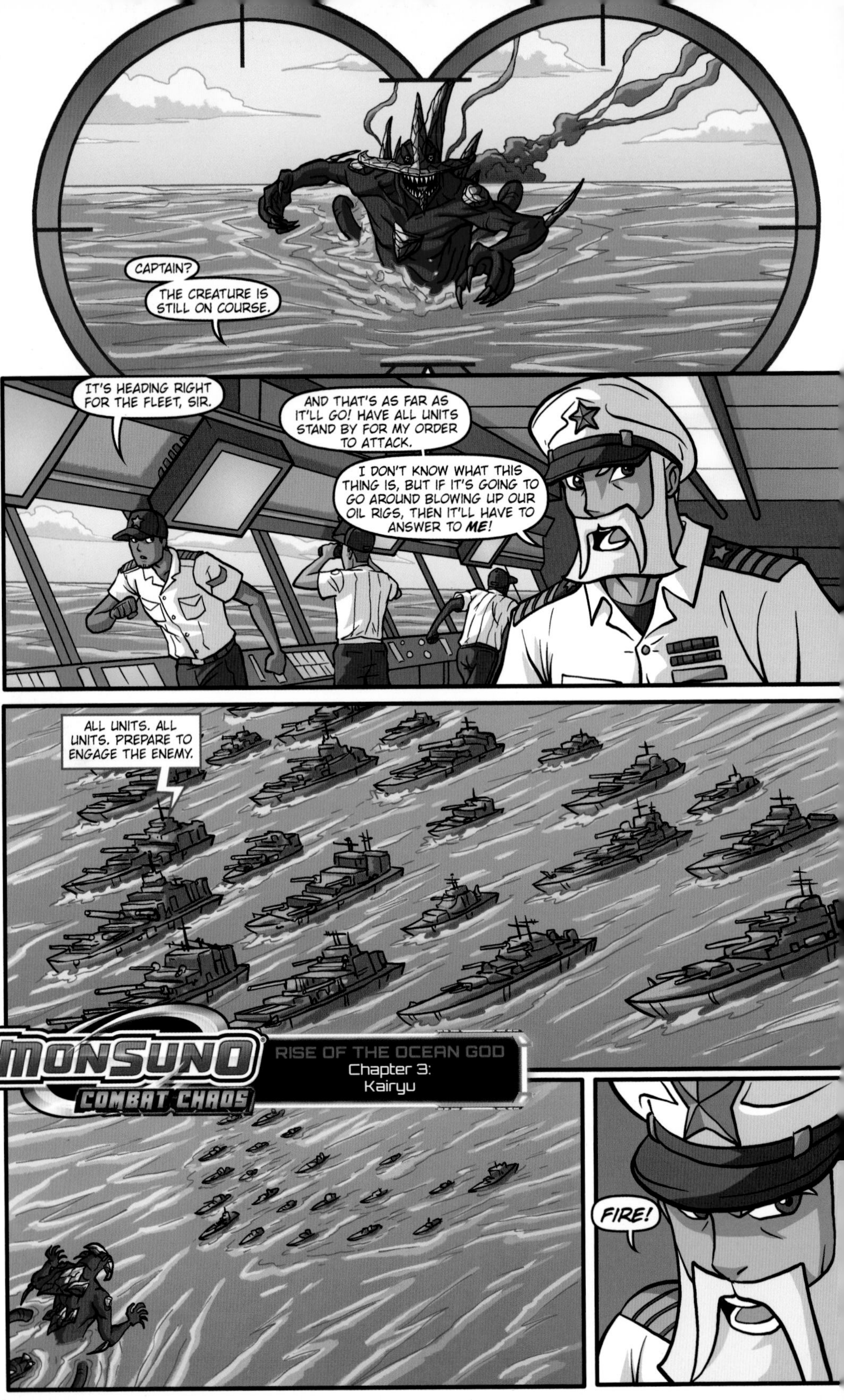
CAPTAIN?
THE CREATURE IS STILL ON COURSE.
IT'S HEADING RIGHT FOR THE FLEET, SIR.
AND THAT'S AS FAR AS IT'LL GO! HAVE ALL UNITS STAND BY FOR MY ORDER TO ATTACK.
I DON'T KNOW WHAT THIS THING IS, BUT IF IT'S GOING TO GO AROUND BLOWING UP OUR OIL RIGS, THEN IT'LL HAVE TO ANSWER TO *ME*!
ALL UNITS. ALL UNITS. PREPARE TO ENGAGE THE ENEMY.
MONSUNO COMBAT CHAOS
RISE OF THE OCEAN GOD
Chapter 3:
Kairyu
FIRE!

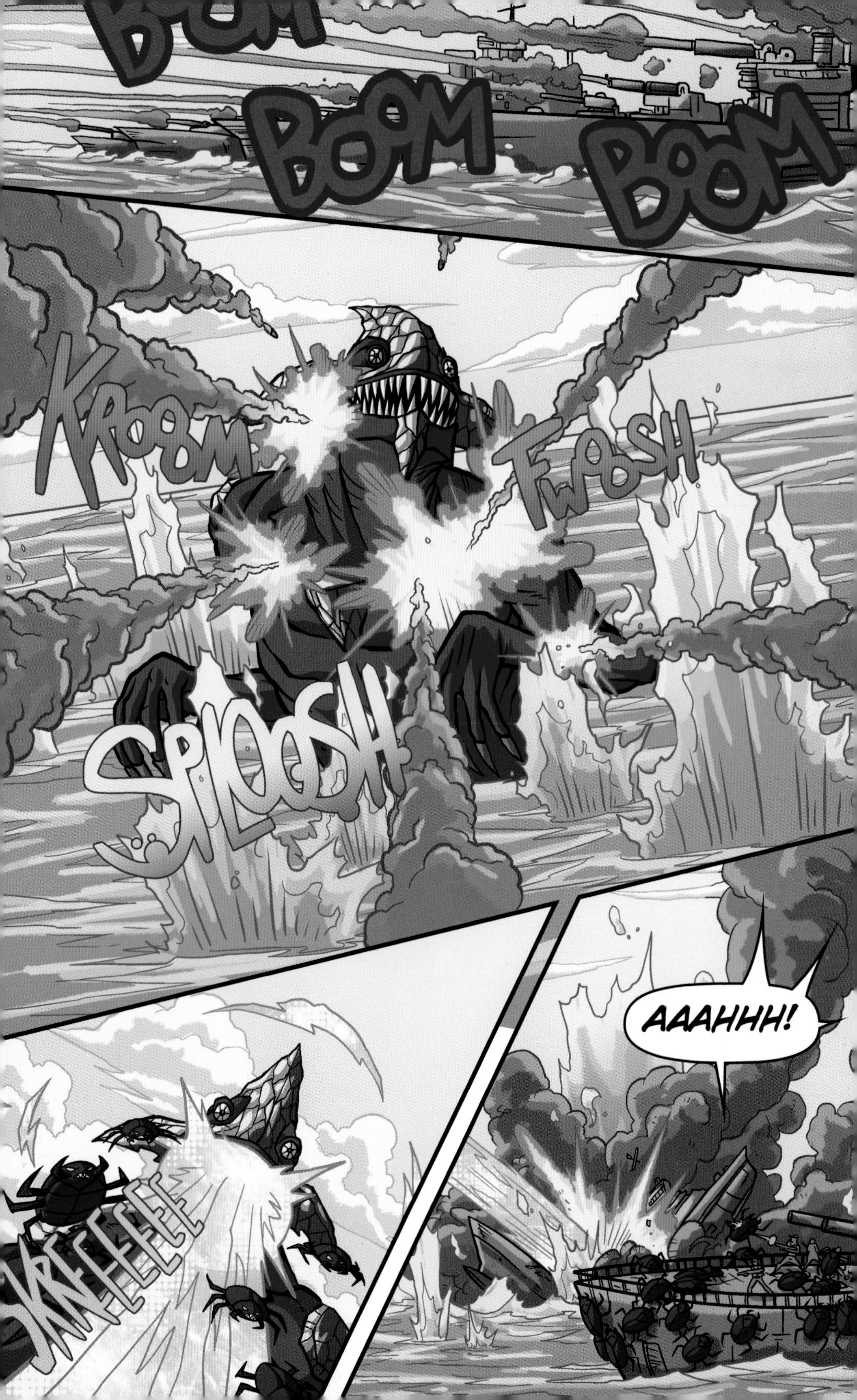
BOOM
BOOM
BOOM
KROOM
FWOOSH
SPLOOSH
SKREEEEE
AAAHHH!

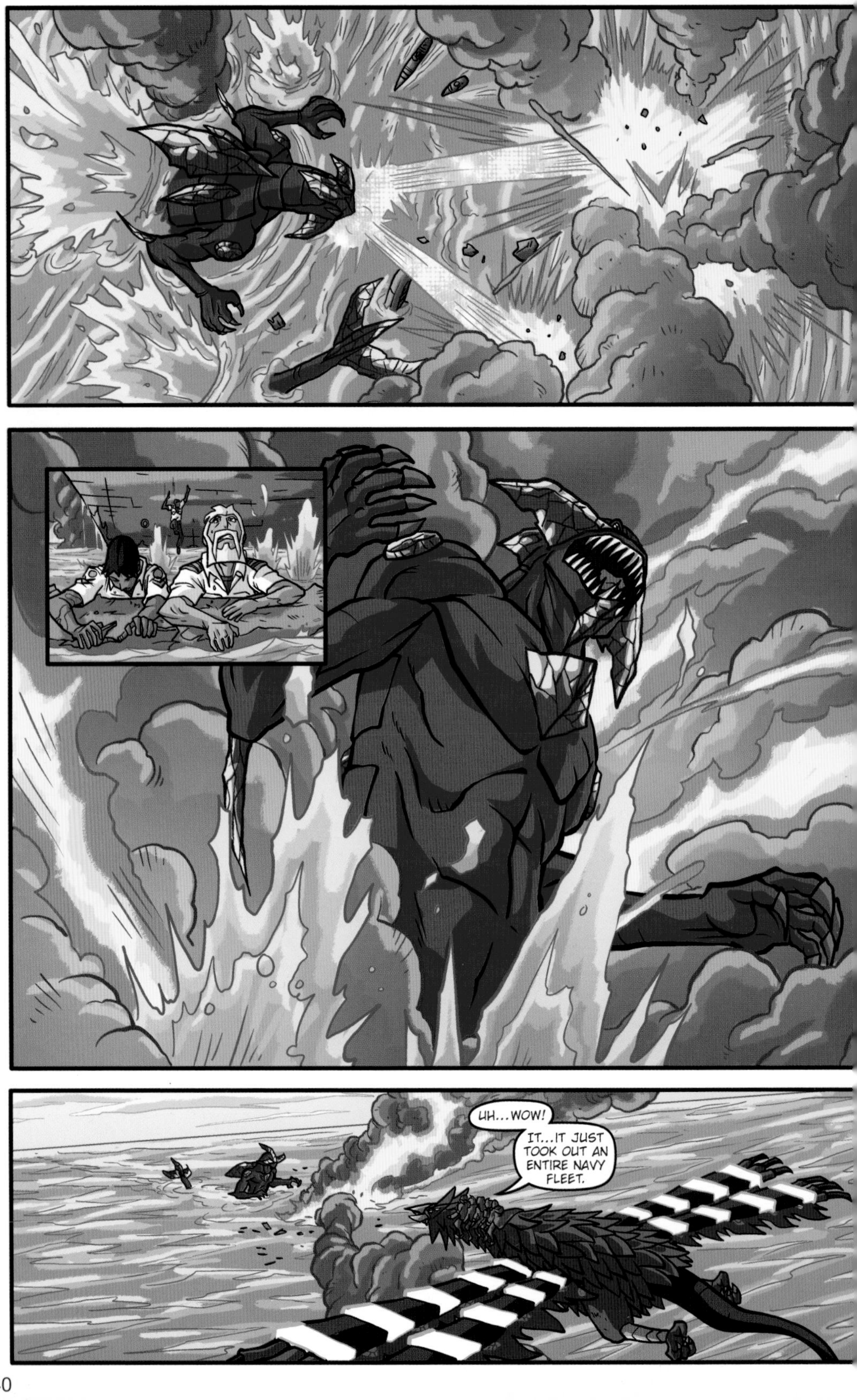
UH...WOW!
IT...IT JUST TOOK OUT AN ENTIRE NAVY FLEET.

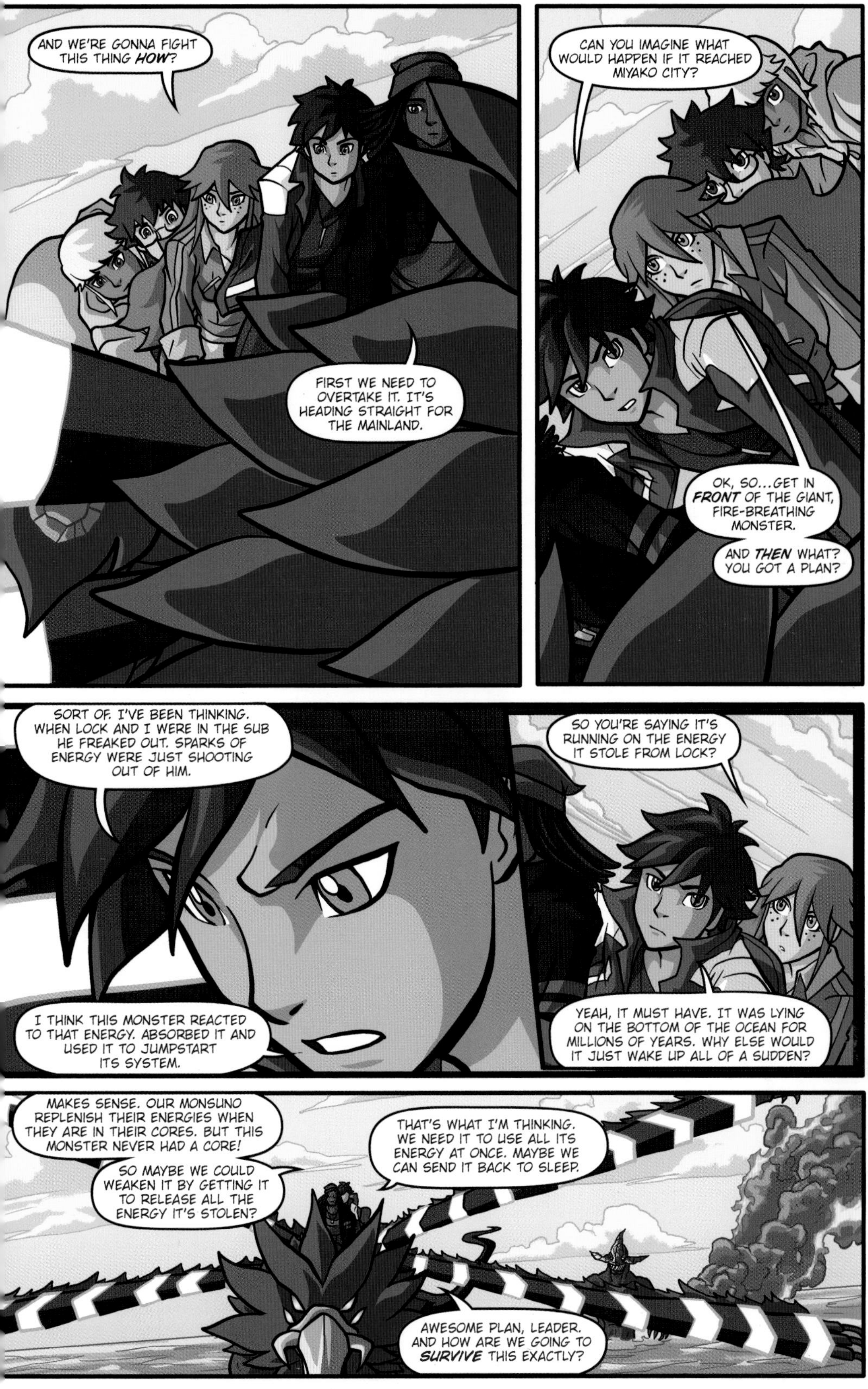
AND WE'RE GONNA FIGHT THIS THING *HOW*?
FIRST WE NEED TO OVERTAKE IT. IT'S HEADING STRAIGHT FOR THE MAINLAND.
CAN YOU IMAGINE WHAT WOULD HAPPEN IF IT REACHED MIYAKO CITY?
OK, SO...GET IN *FRONT* OF THE GIANT, FIRE-BREATHING MONSTER.
AND *THEN* WHAT? YOU GOT A PLAN?
SORT OF. I'VE BEEN THINKING. WHEN LOCK AND I WERE IN THE SUB HE FREAKED OUT. SPARKS OF ENERGY WERE JUST SHOOTING OUT OF HIM.
I THINK THIS MONSTER REACTED TO THAT ENERGY. ABSORBED IT AND USED IT TO JUMPSTART ITS SYSTEM.
SO YOU'RE SAYING IT'S RUNNING ON THE ENERGY IT STOLE FROM LOCK?
YEAH, IT MUST HAVE. IT WAS LYING ON THE BOTTOM OF THE OCEAN FOR MILLIONS OF YEARS. WHY ELSE WOULD IT JUST WAKE UP ALL OF A SUDDEN?
MAKES SENSE. OUR MONSUNO REPLENISH THEIR ENERGIES WHEN THEY ARE IN THEIR CORES. BUT THIS MONSTER NEVER HAD A CORE!
SO MAYBE WE COULD WEAKEN IT BY GETTING IT TO RELEASE ALL THE ENERGY IT'S STOLEN?
THAT'S WHAT I'M THINKING. WE NEED IT TO USE ALL ITS ENERGY AT ONCE. MAYBE WE CAN SEND IT BACK TO SLEEP.
AWESOME PLAN, LEADER. AND HOW ARE WE GOING TO *SURVIVE* THIS EXACTLY?

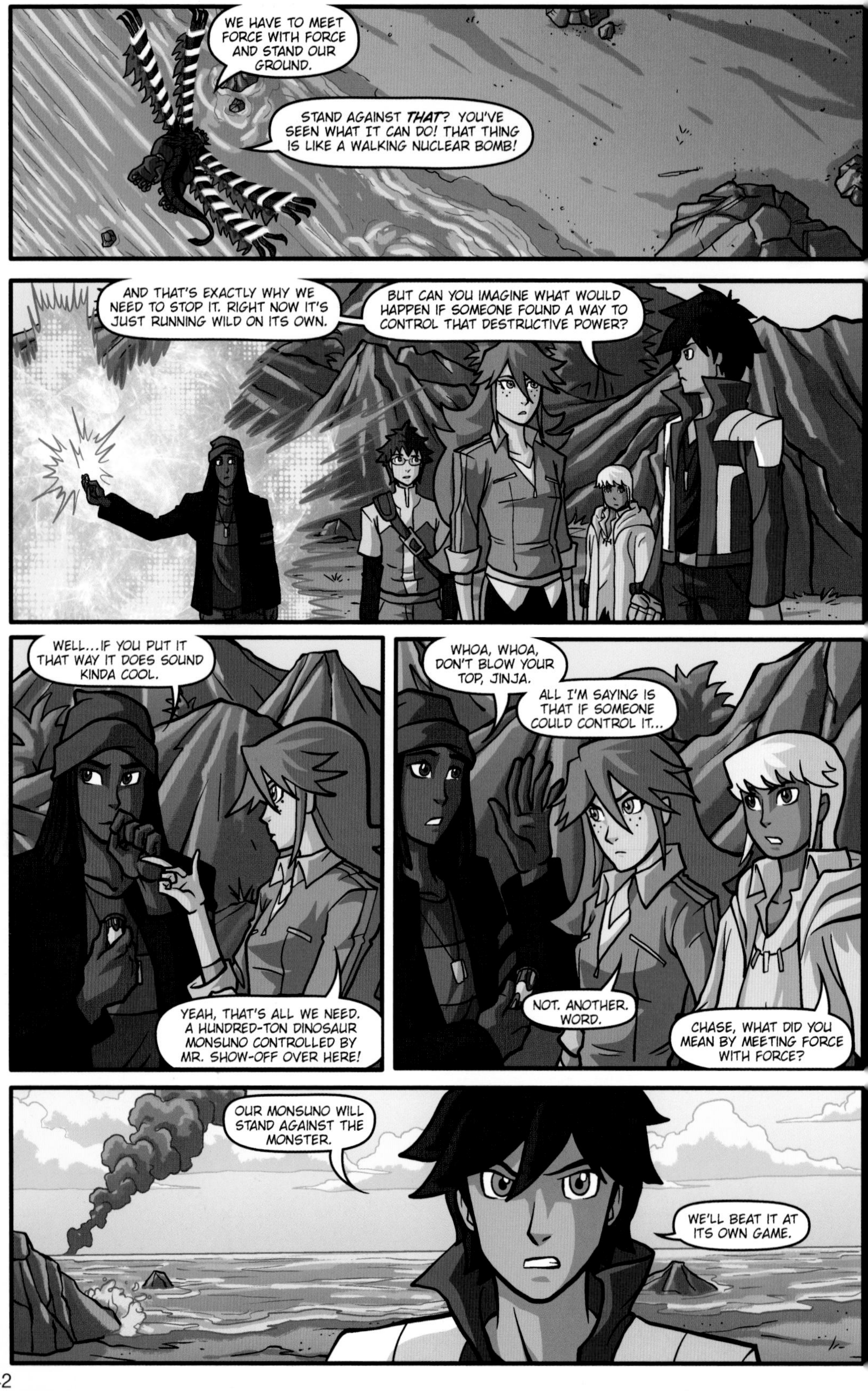
WE HAVE TO MEET FORCE WITH FORCE AND STAND OUR GROUND.
STAND AGAINST *THAT*? YOU'VE SEEN WHAT IT CAN DO! THAT THING IS LIKE A WALKING NUCLEAR BOMB!
AND THAT'S EXACTLY WHY WE NEED TO STOP IT. RIGHT NOW IT'S JUST RUNNING WILD ON ITS OWN.
BUT CAN YOU IMAGINE WHAT WOULD HAPPEN IF SOMEONE FOUND A WAY TO CONTROL THAT DESTRUCTIVE POWER?
WELL...IF YOU PUT IT THAT WAY IT DOES SOUND KINDA COOL.
YEAH, THAT'S ALL WE NEED. A HUNDRED-TON DINOSAUR MONSUNO CONTROLLED BY MR. SHOW-OFF OVER HERE!
WHOA, WHOA, DON'T BLOW YOUR TOP, JINJA.
ALL I'M SAYING IS THAT IF SOMEONE COULD CONTROL IT...
NOT. ANOTHER. WORD.
CHASE, WHAT DID YOU MEAN BY MEETING FORCE WITH FORCE?
OUR MONSUNO WILL STAND AGAINST THE MONSTER.
WE'LL BEAT IT AT ITS OWN GAME.

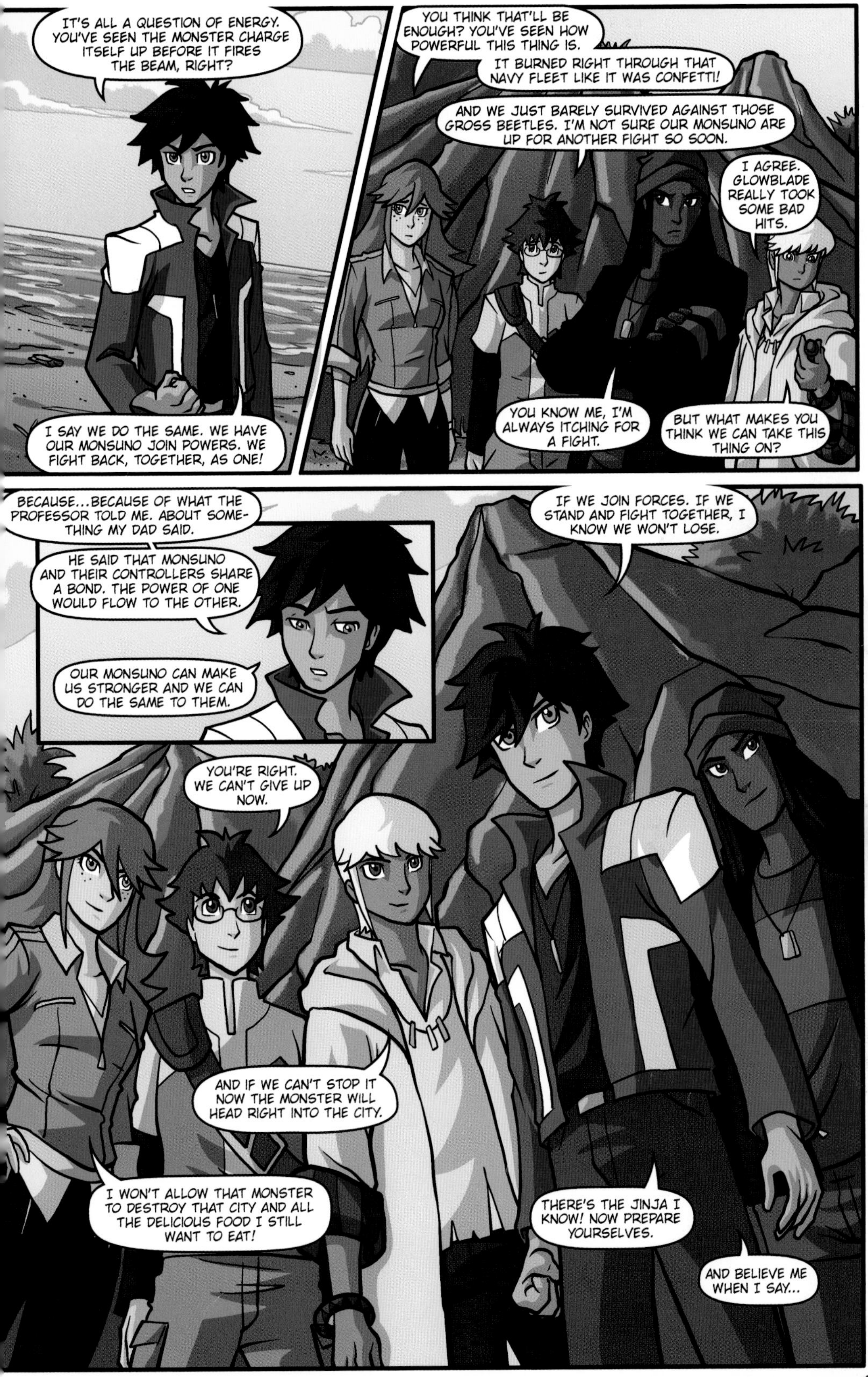
IT'S ALL A QUESTION OF ENERGY. YOU'VE SEEN THE MONSTER CHARGE ITSELF UP BEFORE IT FIRES THE BEAM, RIGHT?
I SAY WE DO THE SAME. WE HAVE OUR MONSUNO JOIN POWERS. WE FIGHT BACK, TOGETHER, AS ONE!
YOU THINK THAT'LL BE ENOUGH? YOU'VE SEEN HOW POWERFUL THIS THING IS.
IT BURNED RIGHT THROUGH THAT NAVY FLEET LIKE IT WAS CONFETTI!
AND WE JUST BARELY SURVIVED AGAINST THOSE GROSS BEETLES. I'M NOT SURE OUR MONSUNO ARE UP FOR ANOTHER FIGHT SO SOON.
I AGREE. GLOWBLADE REALLY TOOK SOME BAD HITS.
YOU KNOW ME, I'M ALWAYS ITCHING FOR A FIGHT.
BUT WHAT MAKES YOU THINK WE CAN TAKE THIS THING ON?
BECAUSE...BECAUSE OF WHAT THE PROFESSOR TOLD ME. ABOUT SOMETHING MY DAD SAID.
HE SAID THAT MONSUNO AND THEIR CONTROLLERS SHARE A BOND. THE POWER OF ONE WOULD FLOW TO THE OTHER.
OUR MONSUNO CAN MAKE US STRONGER AND WE CAN DO THE SAME TO THEM.
IF WE JOIN FORCES. IF WE STAND AND FIGHT TOGETHER, I KNOW WE WON'T LOSE.
YOU'RE RIGHT. WE CAN'T GIVE UP NOW.
AND IF WE CAN'T STOP IT NOW THE MONSTER WILL HEAD RIGHT INTO THE CITY.
I WON'T ALLOW THAT MONSTER TO DESTROY THAT CITY AND ALL THE DELICIOUS FOOD I STILL WANT TO EAT!
THERE'S THE JINJA I KNOW! NOW PREPARE YOURSELVES.
AND BELIEVE ME WHEN I SAY...

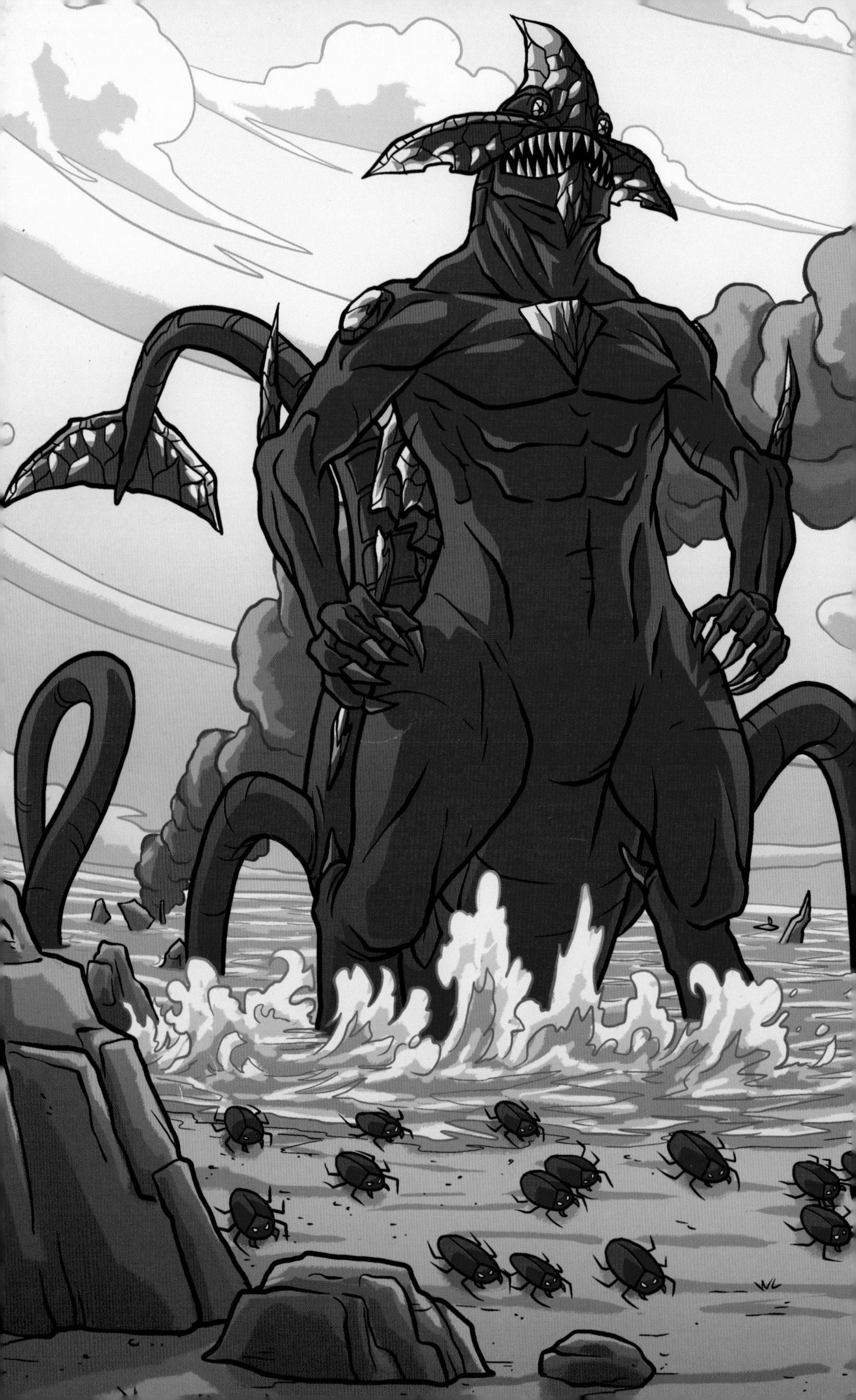

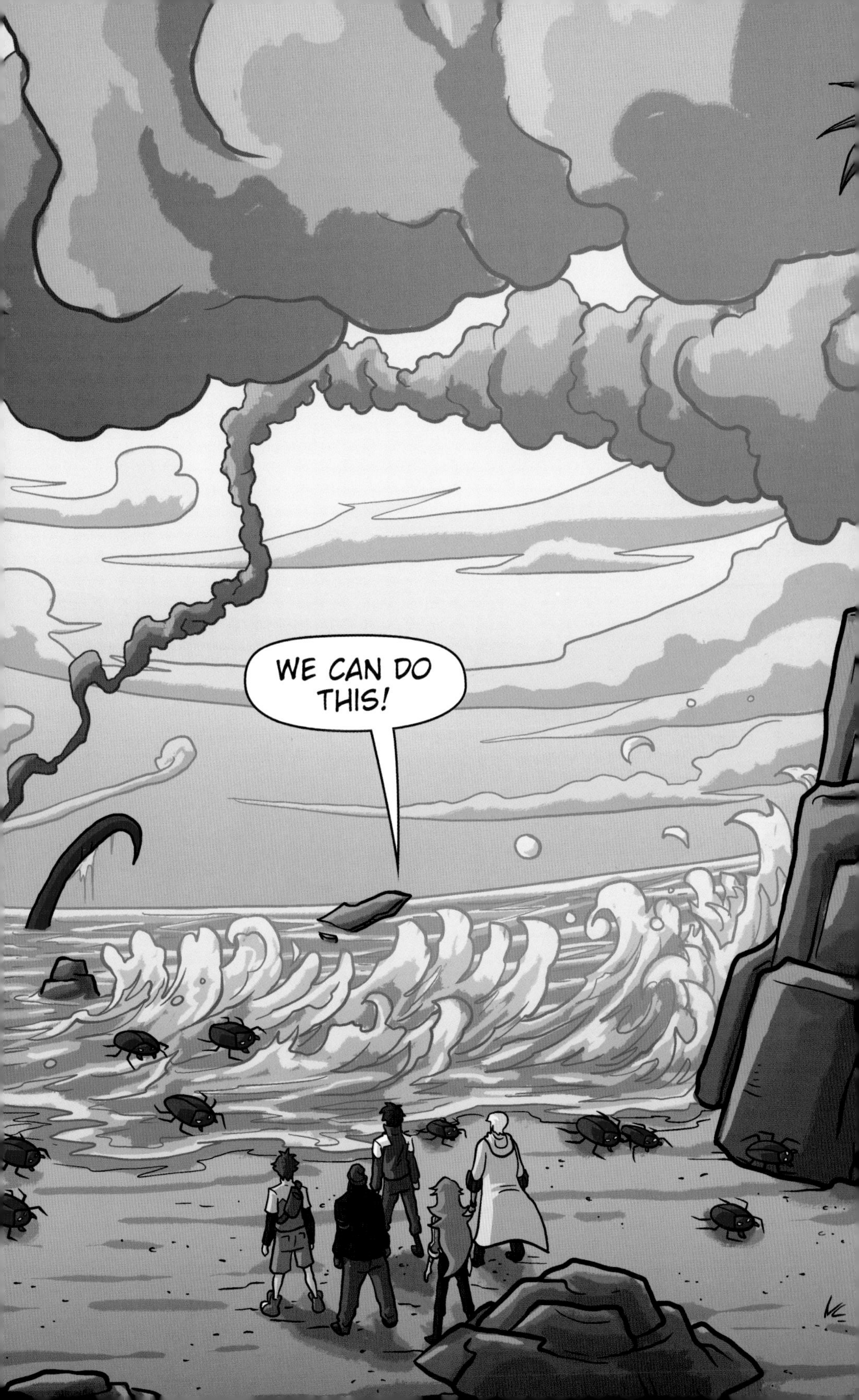
WE CAN DO THIS!

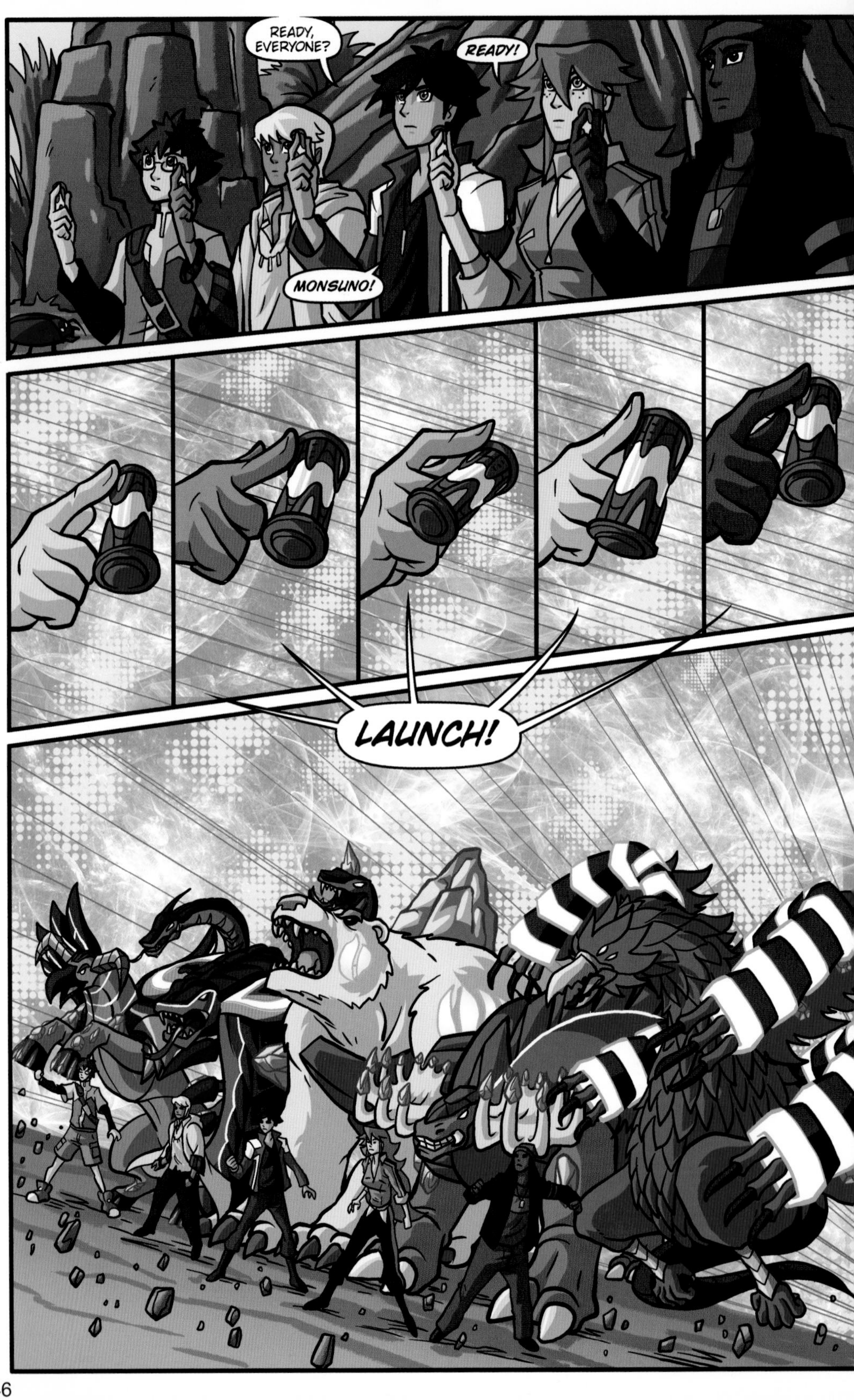
READY, EVERYONE?
READY!
MONSUNO!
LAUNCH!

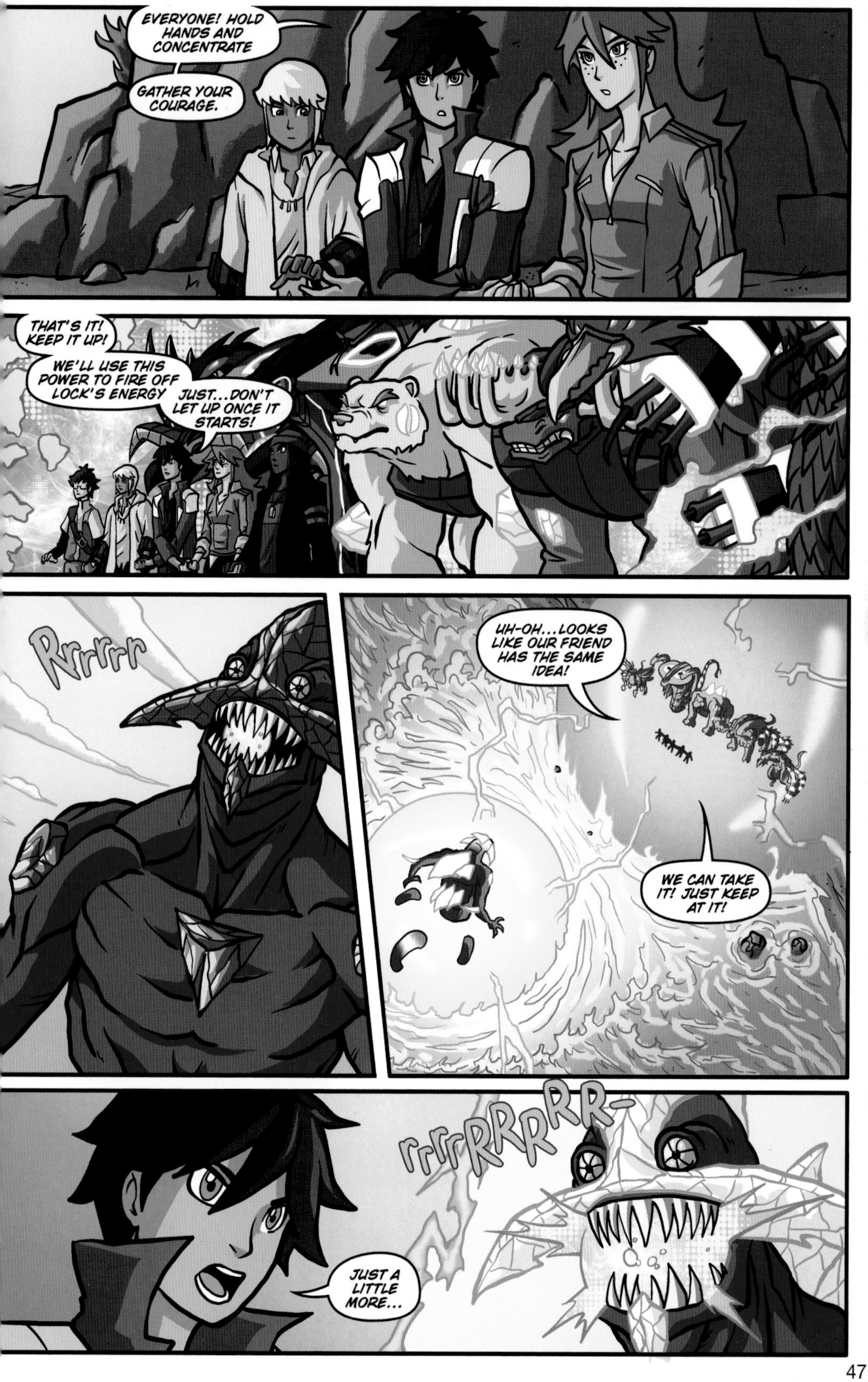
EVERYONE! HOLD HANDS AND CONCENTRATE
GATHER YOUR COURAGE.
THAT'S IT! KEEP IT UP!
WE'LL USE THIS POWER TO FIRE OFF LOCK'S ENERGY
JUST...DON'T LET UP ONCE IT STARTS!
Rrrrrr
UH-OH...LOOKS LIKE OUR FRIEND HAS THE SAME IDEA!
WE CAN TAKE IT! JUST KEEP AT IT!
rrrrRRRRR-
JUST A LITTLE MORE...

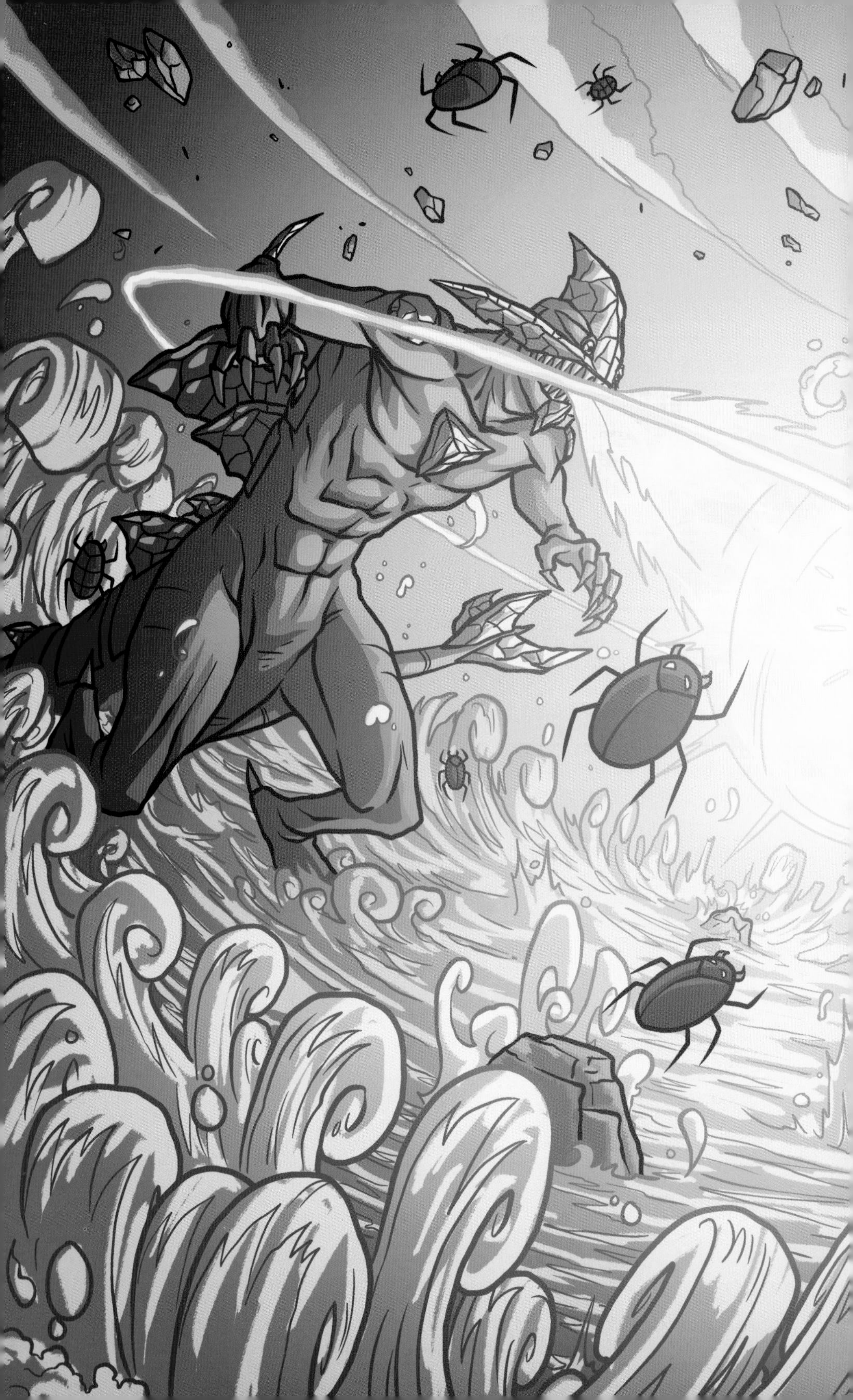

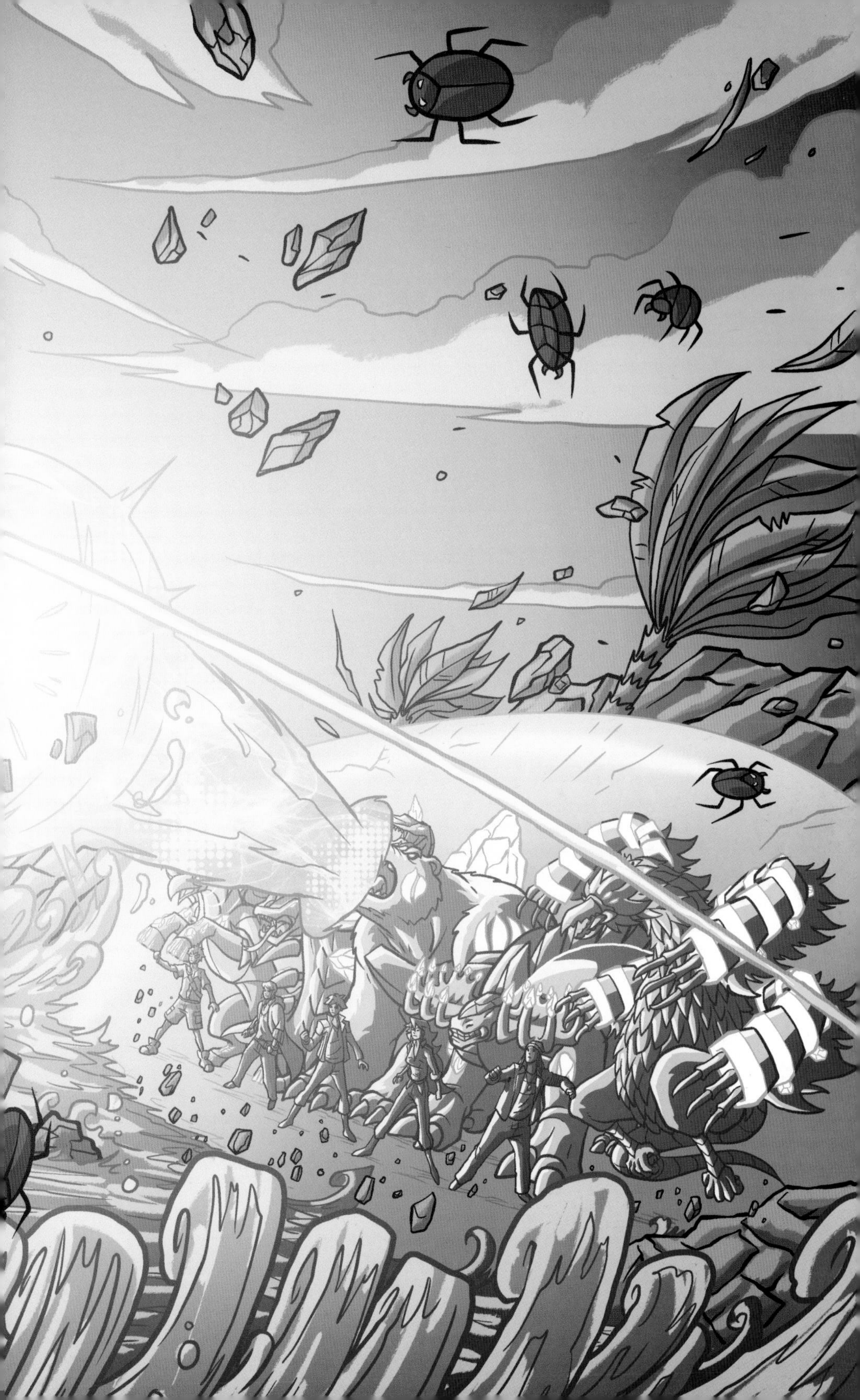

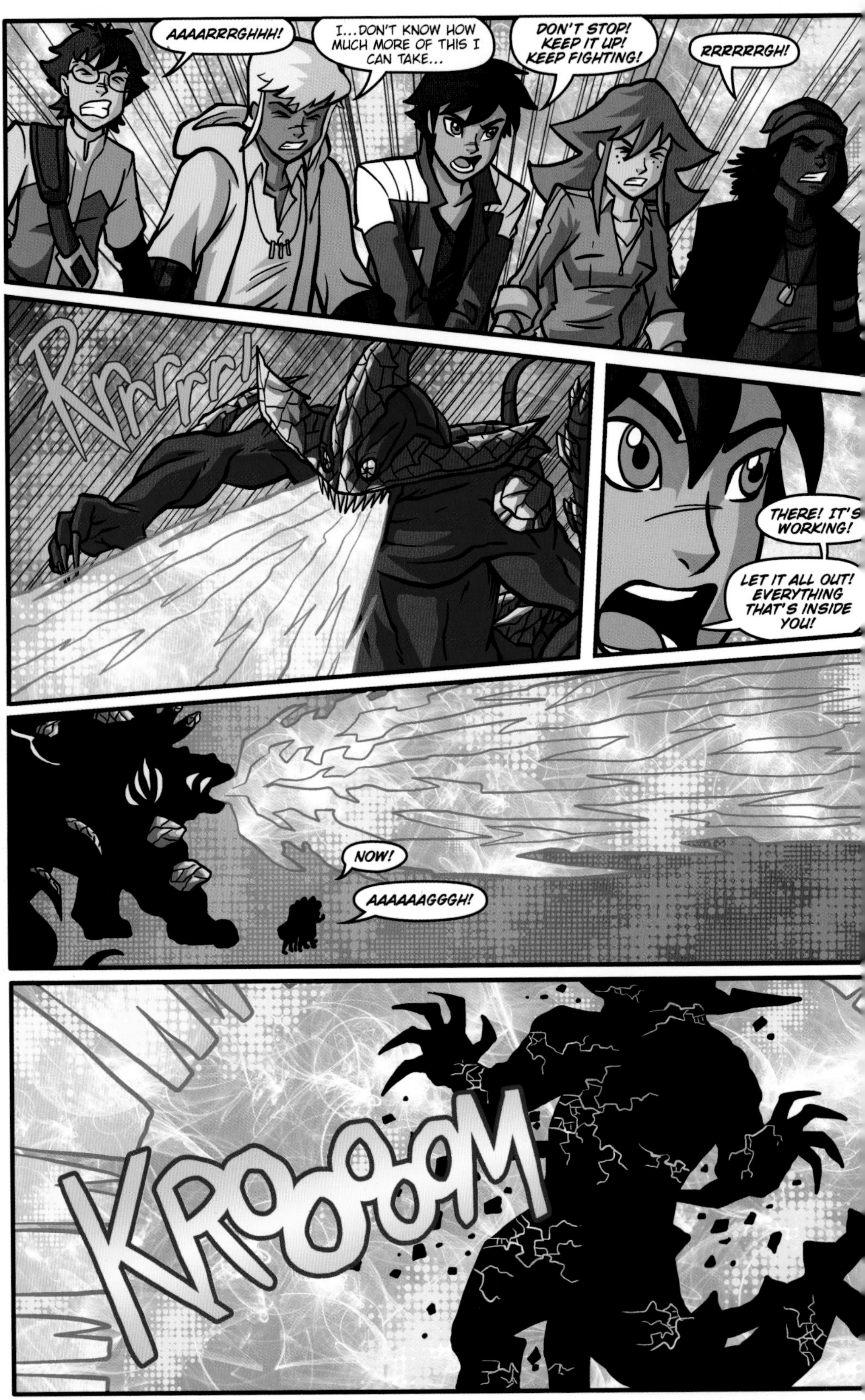
AAAARRRGHHH!
I...DON'T KNOW HOW MUCH MORE OF THIS I CAN TAKE...
DON'T STOP! KEEP IT UP! KEEP FIGHTING!
RRRRRRGH!
Rrrrrrrl
THERE! IT'S WORKING!
LET IT ALL OUT! EVERYTHING THAT'S INSIDE YOU!
NOW!
AAAAAAGGGH!
KROOOOM

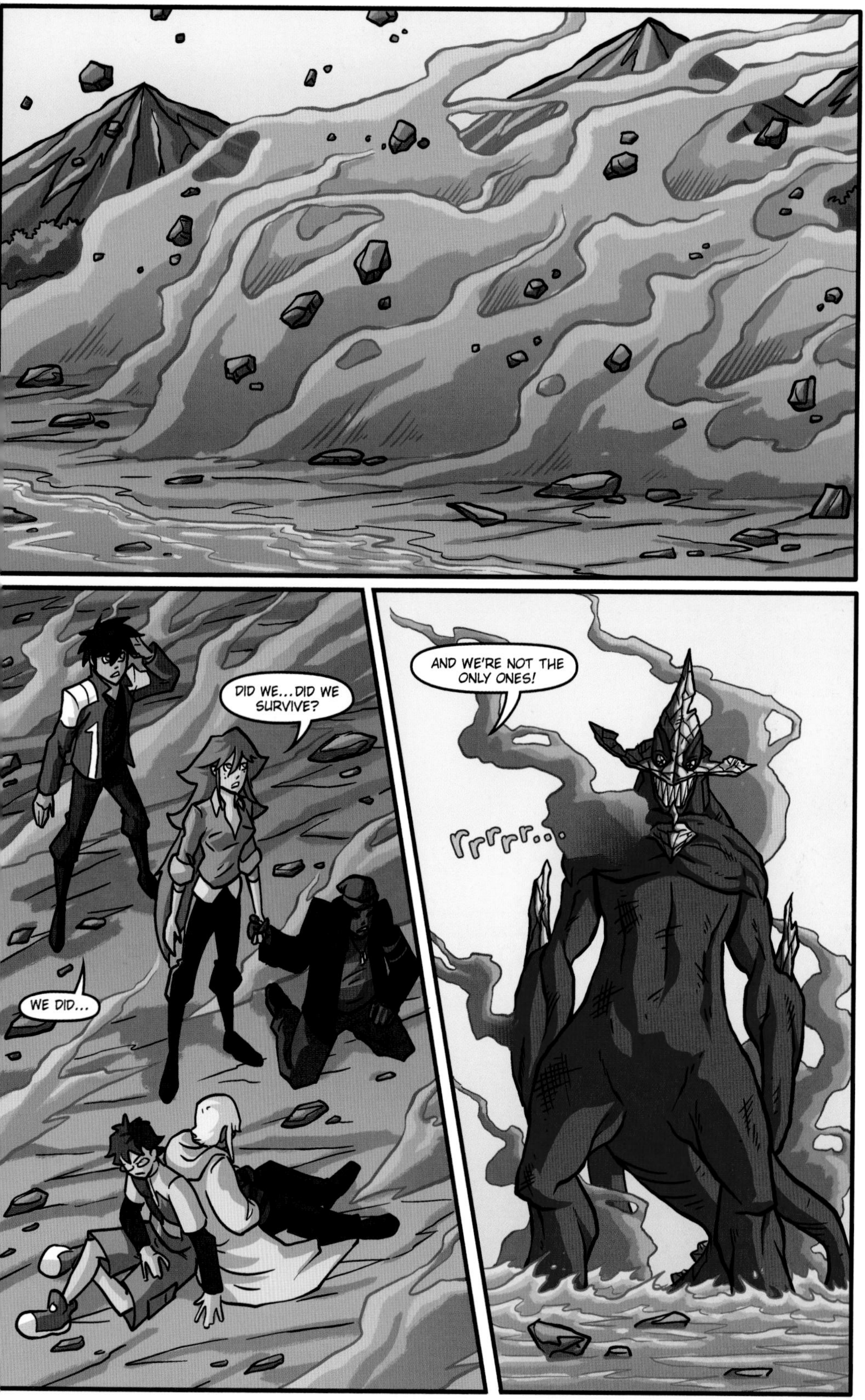
DID WE...DID WE SURVIVE?
WE DID...
AND WE'RE NOT THE ONLY ONES!
rrrrr...

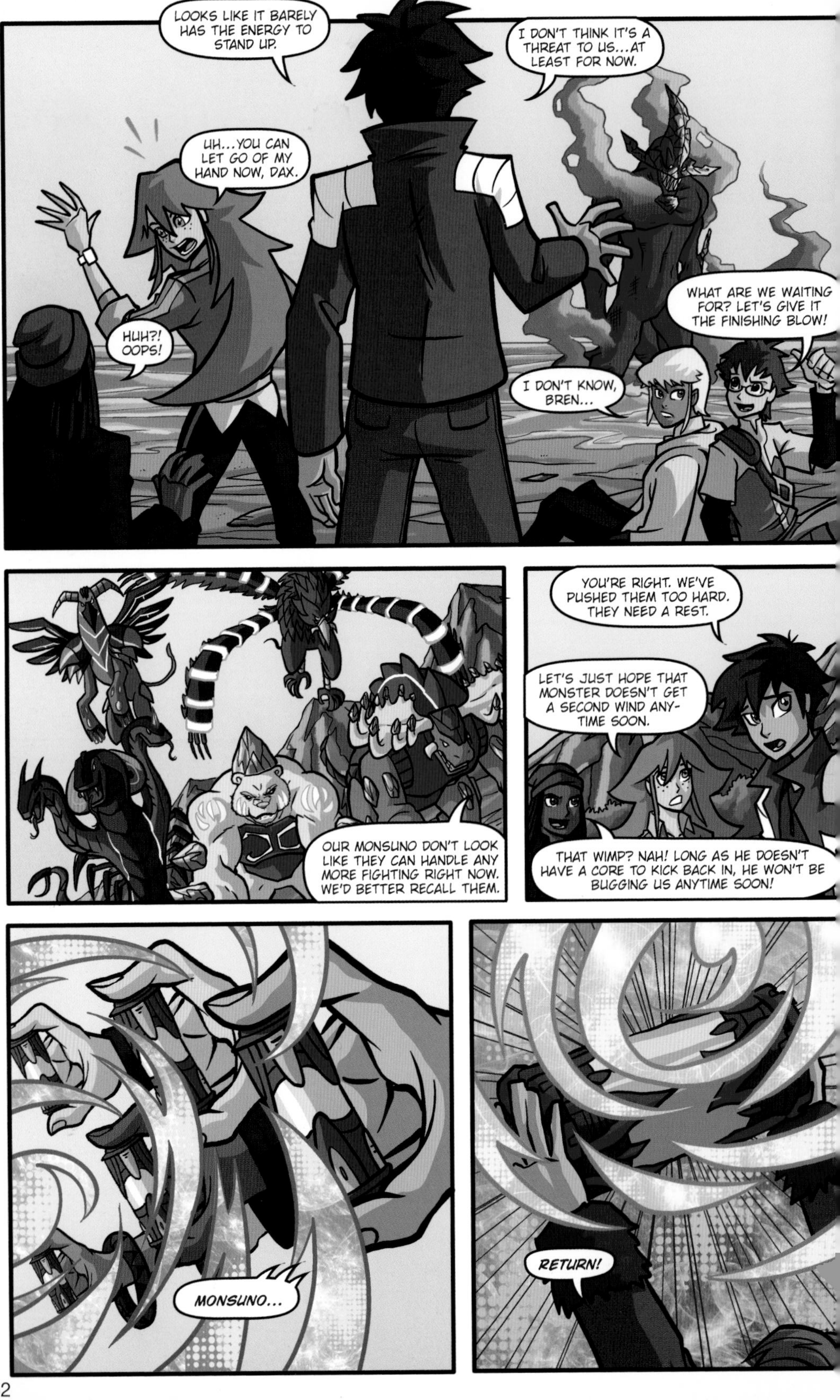

LOOKS LIKE IT BARELY HAS THE ENERGY TO STAND UP.
I DON'T THINK IT'S A THREAT TO US...AT LEAST FOR NOW.
UH...YOU CAN LET GO OF MY HAND NOW, DAX.
HUH?! OOPS!
WHAT ARE WE WAITING FOR? LET'S GIVE IT THE FINISHING BLOW!
I DON'T KNOW, BREN...
OUR MONSUNO DON'T LOOK LIKE THEY CAN HANDLE ANY MORE FIGHTING RIGHT NOW. WE'D BETTER RECALL THEM.
YOU'RE RIGHT. WE'VE PUSHED THEM TOO HARD. THEY NEED A REST.
LET'S JUST HOPE THAT MONSTER DOESN'T GET A SECOND WIND ANY-TIME SOON.
THAT WIMP? NAH! LONG AS HE DOESN'T HAVE A CORE TO KICK BACK IN, HE WON'T BE BUGGING US ANYTIME SOON!
MONSUNO...
RETURN!

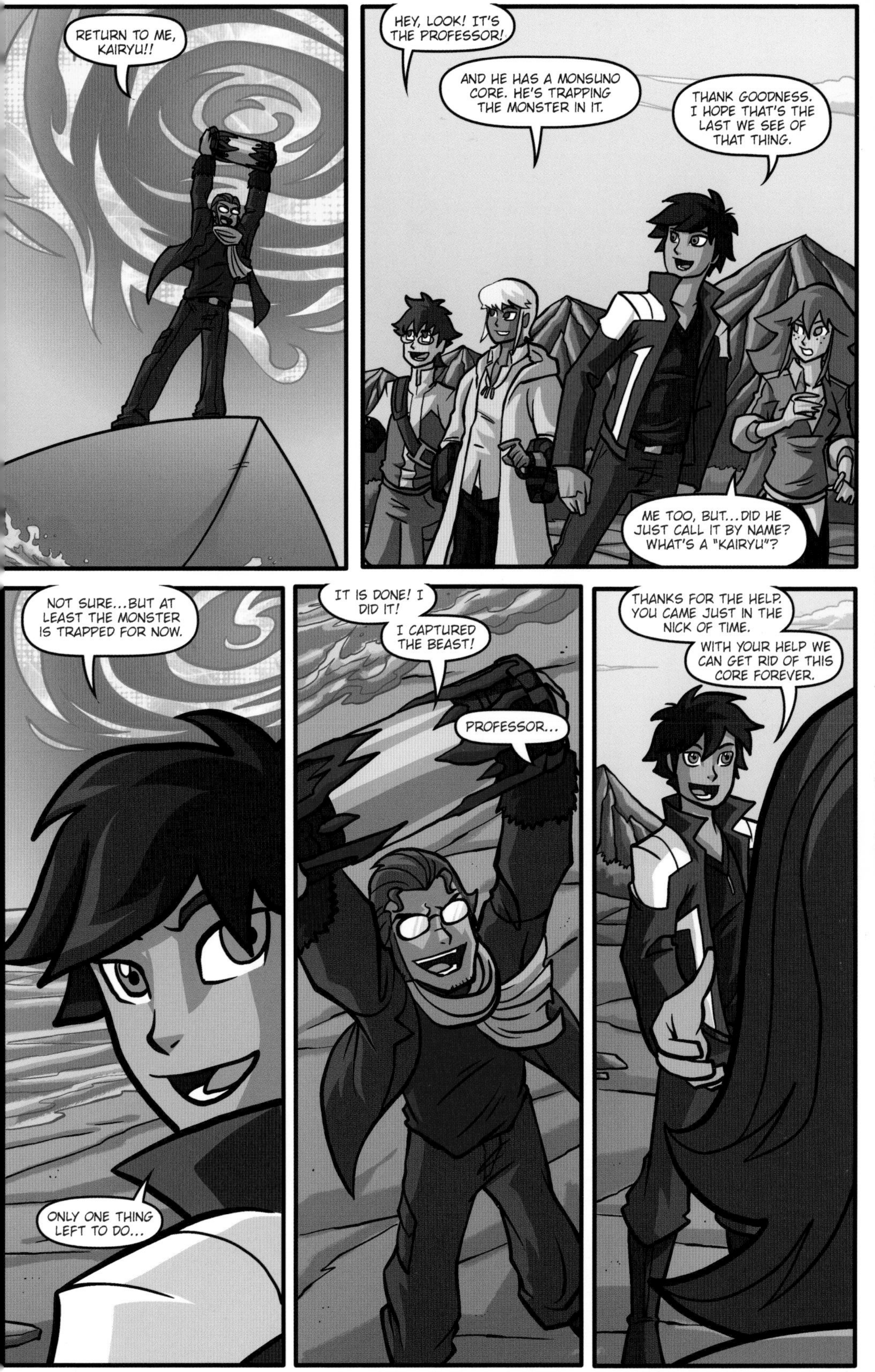
RETURN TO ME, KAIRYU!!
HEY, LOOK! IT'S THE PROFESSOR!
AND HE HAS A MONSUNO CORE. HE'S TRAPPING THE MONSTER IN IT.
THANK GOODNESS. I HOPE THAT'S THE LAST WE SEE OF THAT THING.
ME TOO, BUT...DID HE JUST CALL IT BY NAME? WHAT'S A "KAIRYU"?
NOT SURE...BUT AT LEAST THE MONSTER IS TRAPPED FOR NOW.
ONLY ONE THING LEFT TO DO...
IT IS DONE! I DID IT!
I CAPTURED THE BEAST!
PROFESSOR...
THANKS FOR THE HELP. YOU CAME JUST IN THE NICK OF TIME.
WITH YOUR HELP WE CAN GET RID OF THIS CORE FOREVER.

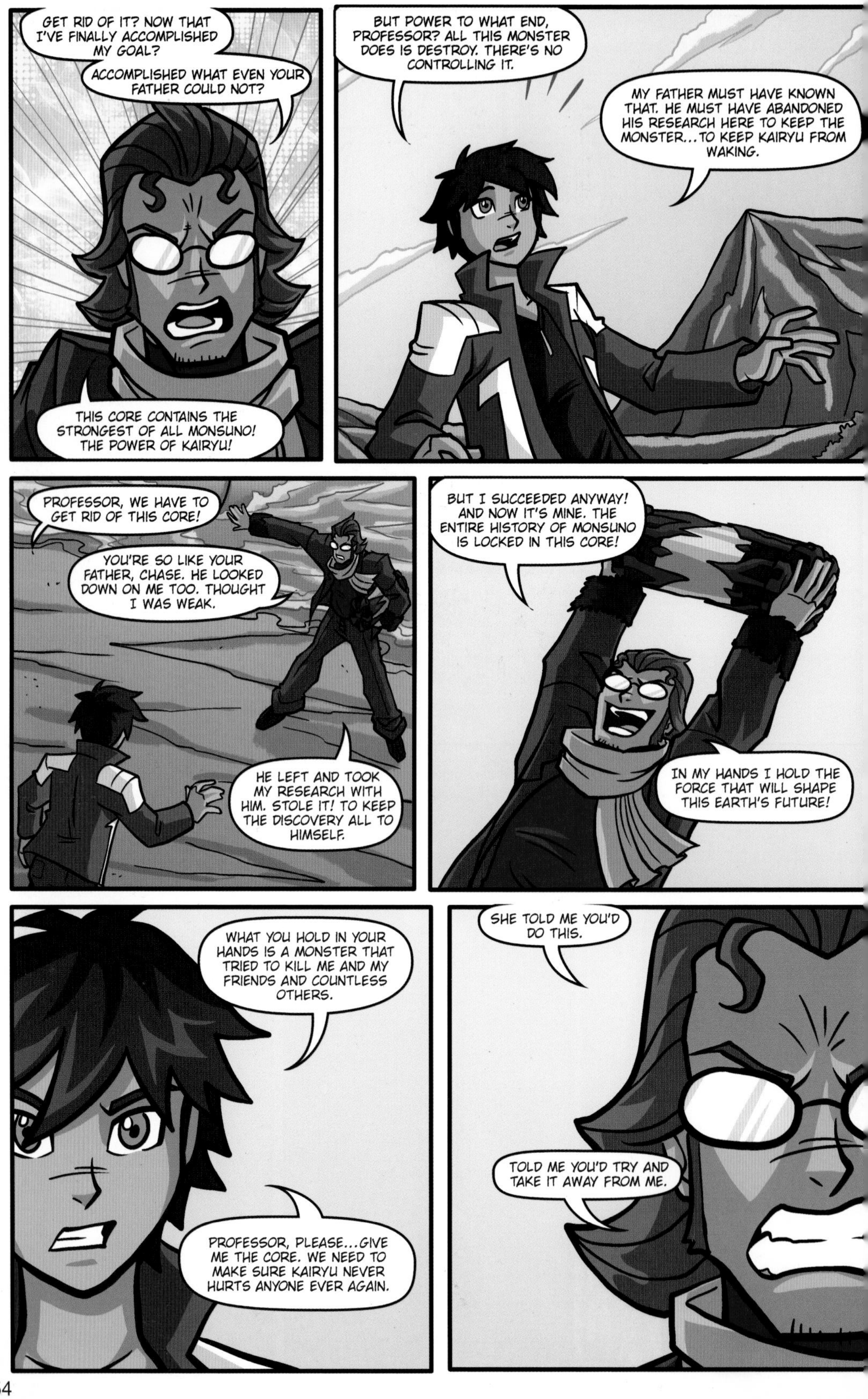
GET RID OF IT? NOW THAT I'VE FINALLY ACCOMPLISHED MY GOAL?
ACCOMPLISHED WHAT EVEN YOUR FATHER COULD NOT?
THIS CORE CONTAINS THE STRONGEST OF ALL MONSUNO! THE POWER OF KAIRYU!
BUT POWER TO WHAT END, PROFESSOR? ALL THIS MONSTER DOES IS DESTROY. THERE'S NO CONTROLLING IT.
MY FATHER MUST HAVE KNOWN THAT. HE MUST HAVE ABANDONED HIS RESEARCH HERE TO KEEP THE MONSTER...TO KEEP KAIRYU FROM WAKING.
PROFESSOR, WE HAVE TO GET RID OF THIS CORE!
YOU'RE SO LIKE YOUR FATHER, CHASE. HE LOOKED DOWN ON ME TOO. THOUGHT I WAS WEAK.
HE LEFT AND TOOK MY RESEARCH WITH HIM. STOLE IT! TO KEEP THE DISCOVERY ALL TO HIMSELF.
BUT I SUCCEEDED ANYWAY! AND NOW IT'S MINE. THE ENTIRE HISTORY OF MONSUNO IS LOCKED IN THIS CORE!
IN MY HANDS I HOLD THE FORCE THAT WILL SHAPE THIS EARTH'S FUTURE!
WHAT YOU HOLD IN YOUR HANDS IS A MONSTER THAT TRIED TO KILL ME AND MY FRIENDS AND COUNTLESS OTHERS.
PROFESSOR, PLEASE...GIVE ME THE CORE. WE NEED TO MAKE SURE KAIRYU NEVER HURTS ANYONE EVER AGAIN.
SHE TOLD ME YOU'D DO THIS.
TOLD ME YOU'D TRY AND TAKE IT AWAY FROM ME.

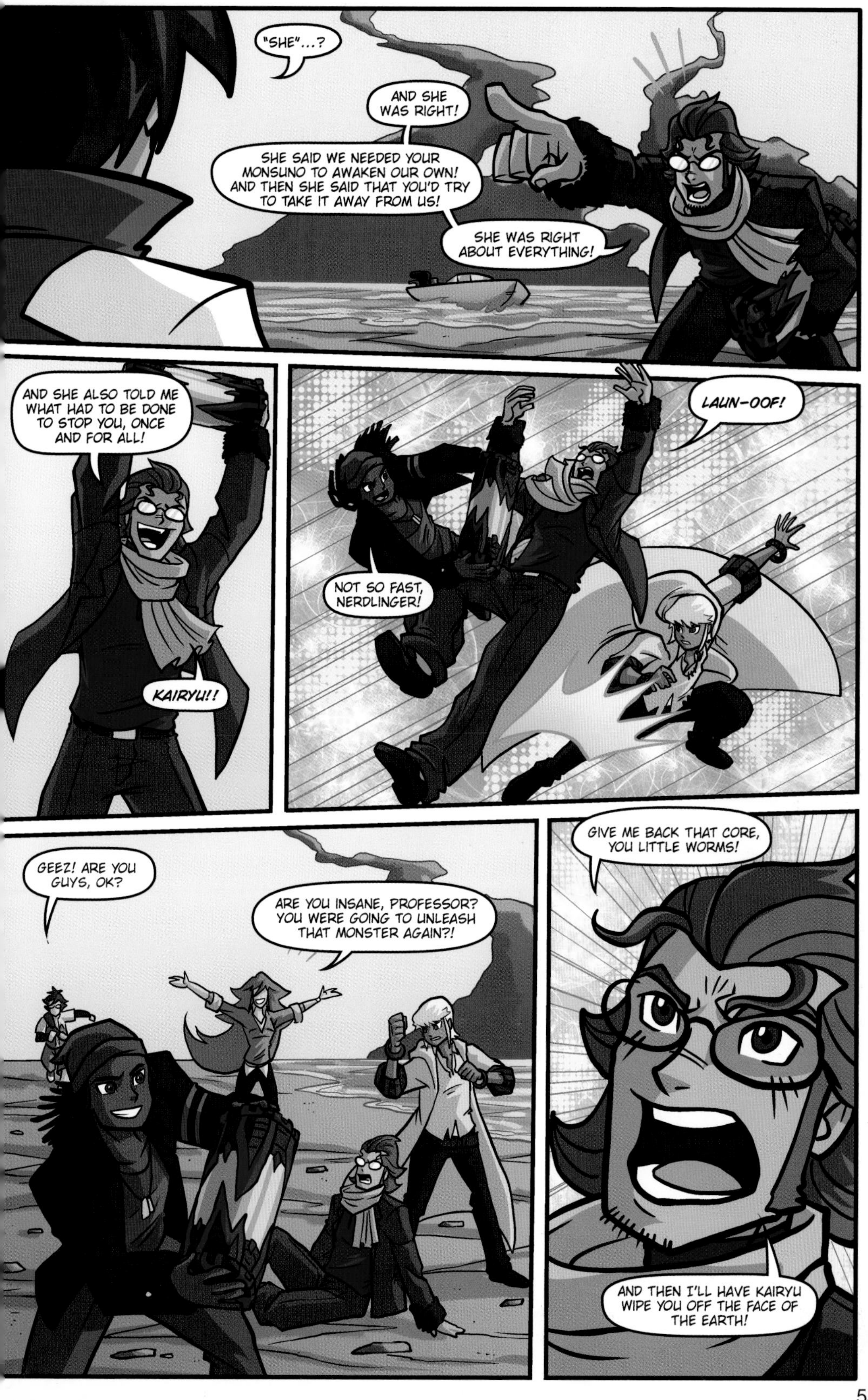
"SHE"...?
AND SHE WAS RIGHT!
SHE SAID WE NEEDED YOUR MONSUNO TO AWAKEN OUR OWN! AND THEN SHE SAID THAT YOU'D TRY TO TAKE IT AWAY FROM US!
SHE WAS RIGHT ABOUT EVERYTHING!
AND SHE ALSO TOLD ME WHAT HAD TO BE DONE TO STOP YOU, ONCE AND FOR ALL!
KAIRYU!!
LAUN-OOF!
NOT SO FAST, NERDLINGER!
GEEZ! ARE YOU GUYS, OK?
ARE YOU INSANE, PROFESSOR? YOU WERE GOING TO UNLEASH THAT MONSTER AGAIN?!
GIVE ME BACK THAT CORE, YOU LITTLE WORMS!
AND THEN I'LL HAVE KAIRYU WIPE YOU OFF THE FACE OF THE EARTH!

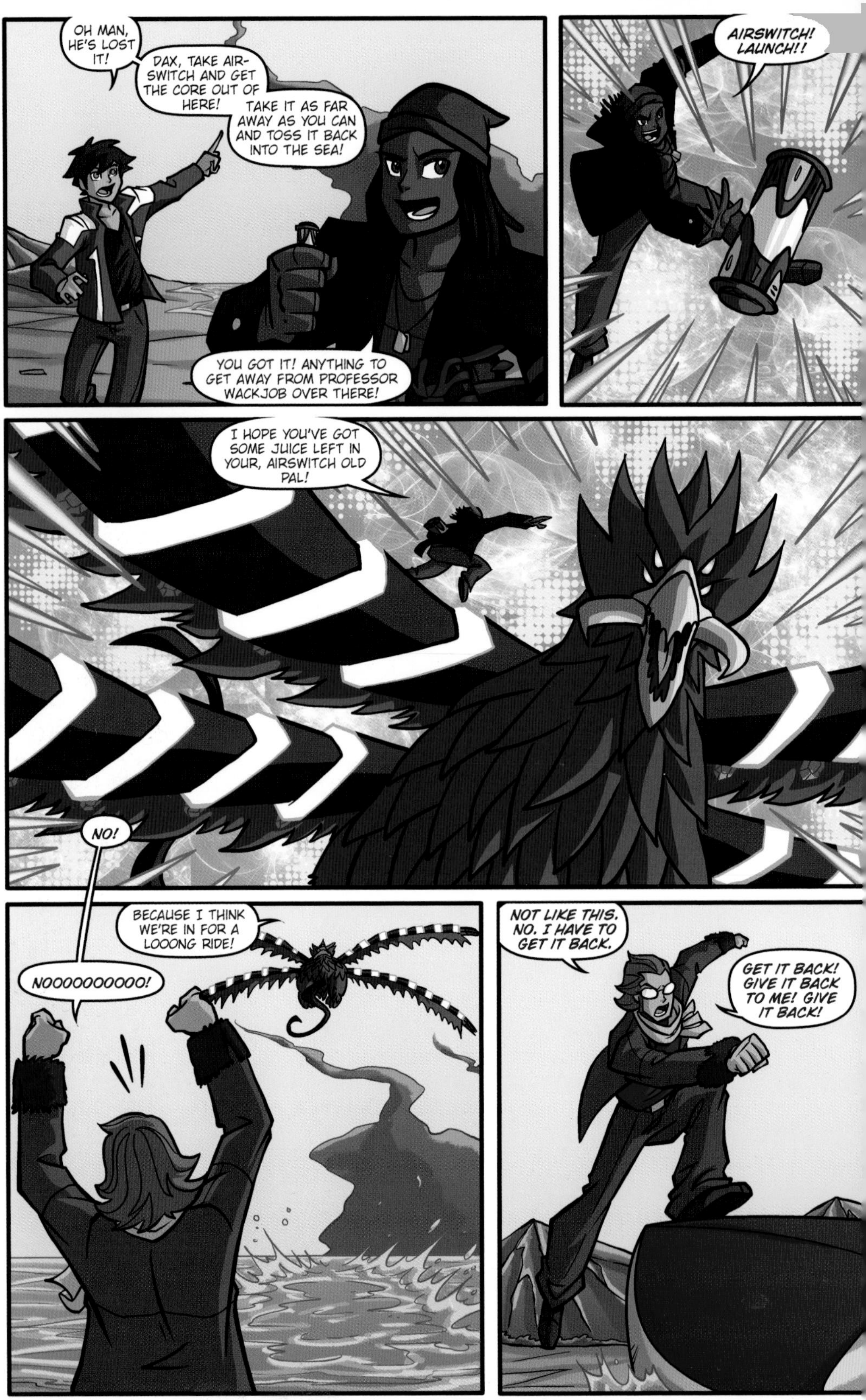
OH MAN, HE'S LOST IT!
DAX, TAKE AIR-SWITCH AND GET THE CORE OUT OF HERE!
TAKE IT AS FAR AWAY AS YOU CAN AND TOSS IT BACK INTO THE SEA!
YOU GOT IT! ANYTHING TO GET AWAY FROM PROFESSOR WACKJOB OVER THERE!
AIRSWITCH! LAUNCH!!
I HOPE YOU'VE GOT SOME JUICE LEFT IN YOUR, AIRSWITCH OLD PAL!
NO!
BECAUSE I THINK WE'RE IN FOR A LOOONG RIDE!
NOOOOOOOOOO!
NOT LIKE THIS. NO. I HAVE TO GET IT BACK.
GET IT BACK! GIVE IT BACK TO ME! GIVE IT BACK!

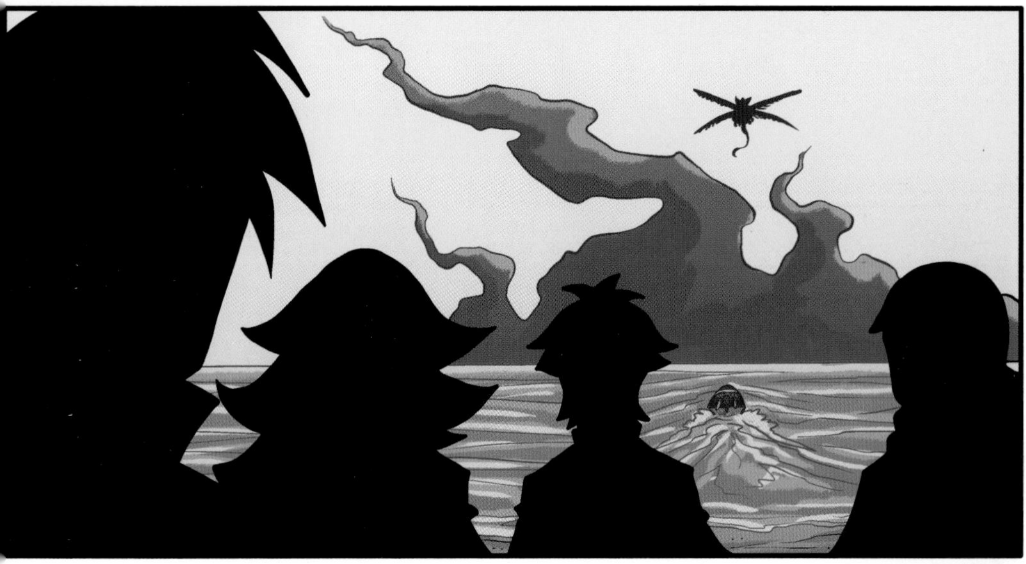

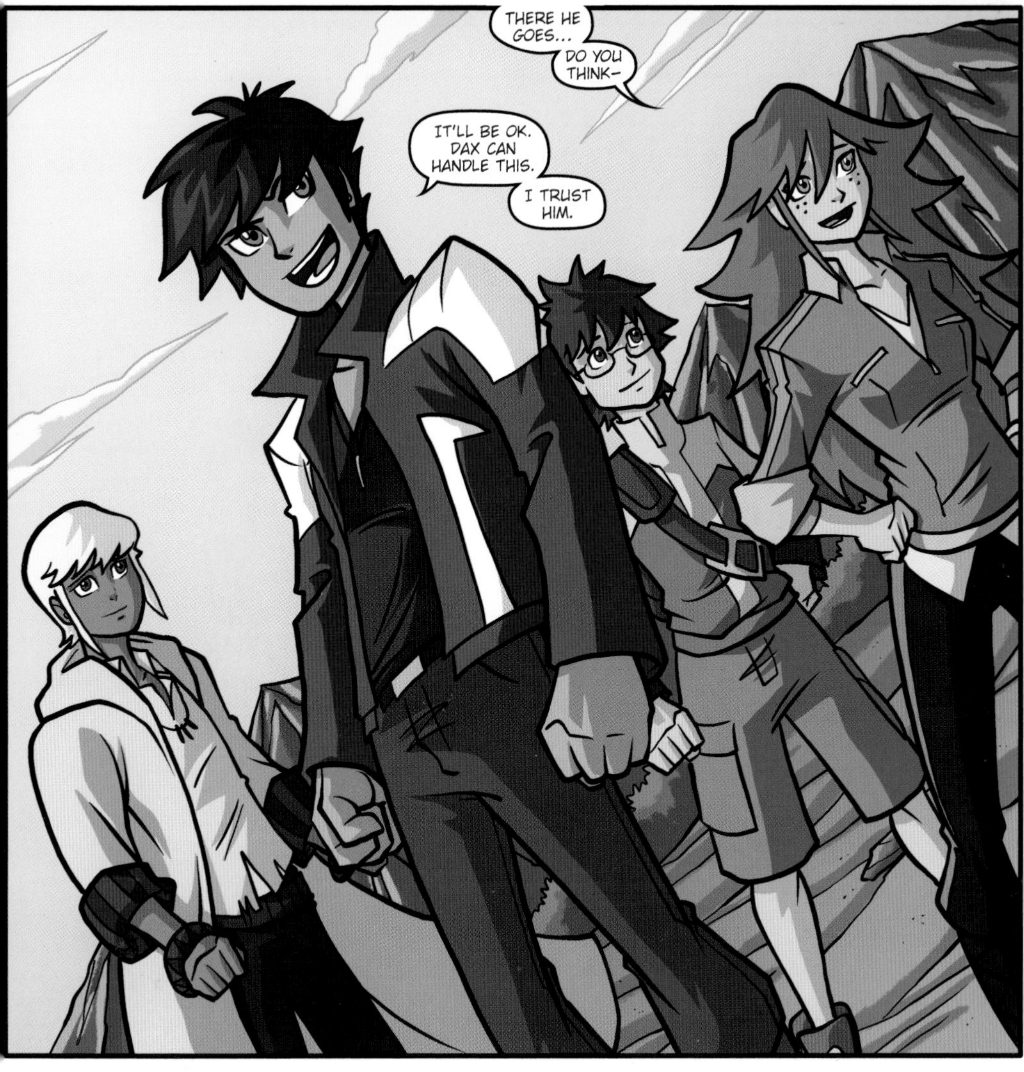
THERE HE GOES...
DO YOU THINK–
IT'LL BE OK. DAX CAN HANDLE THIS.
I TRUST HIM.

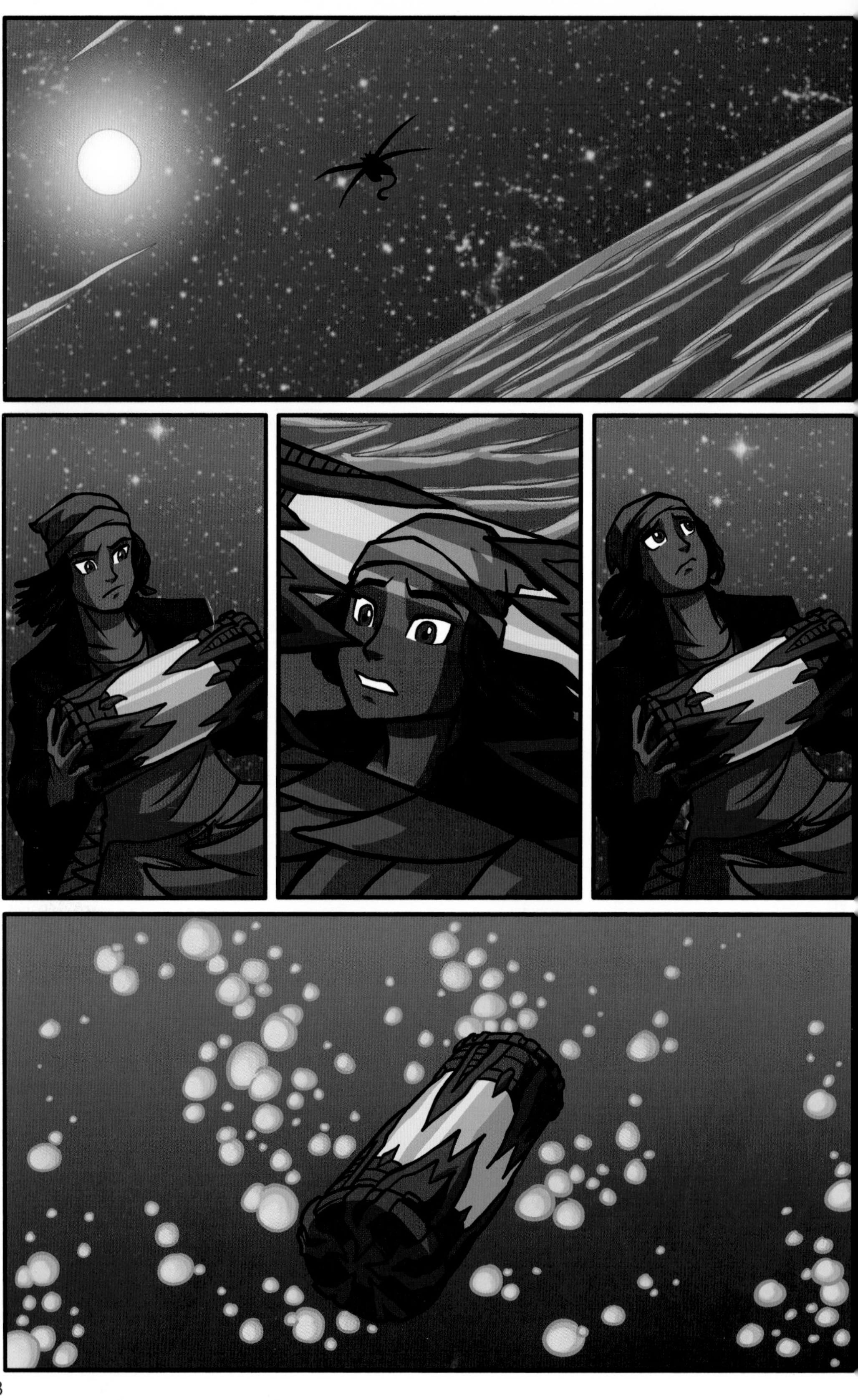

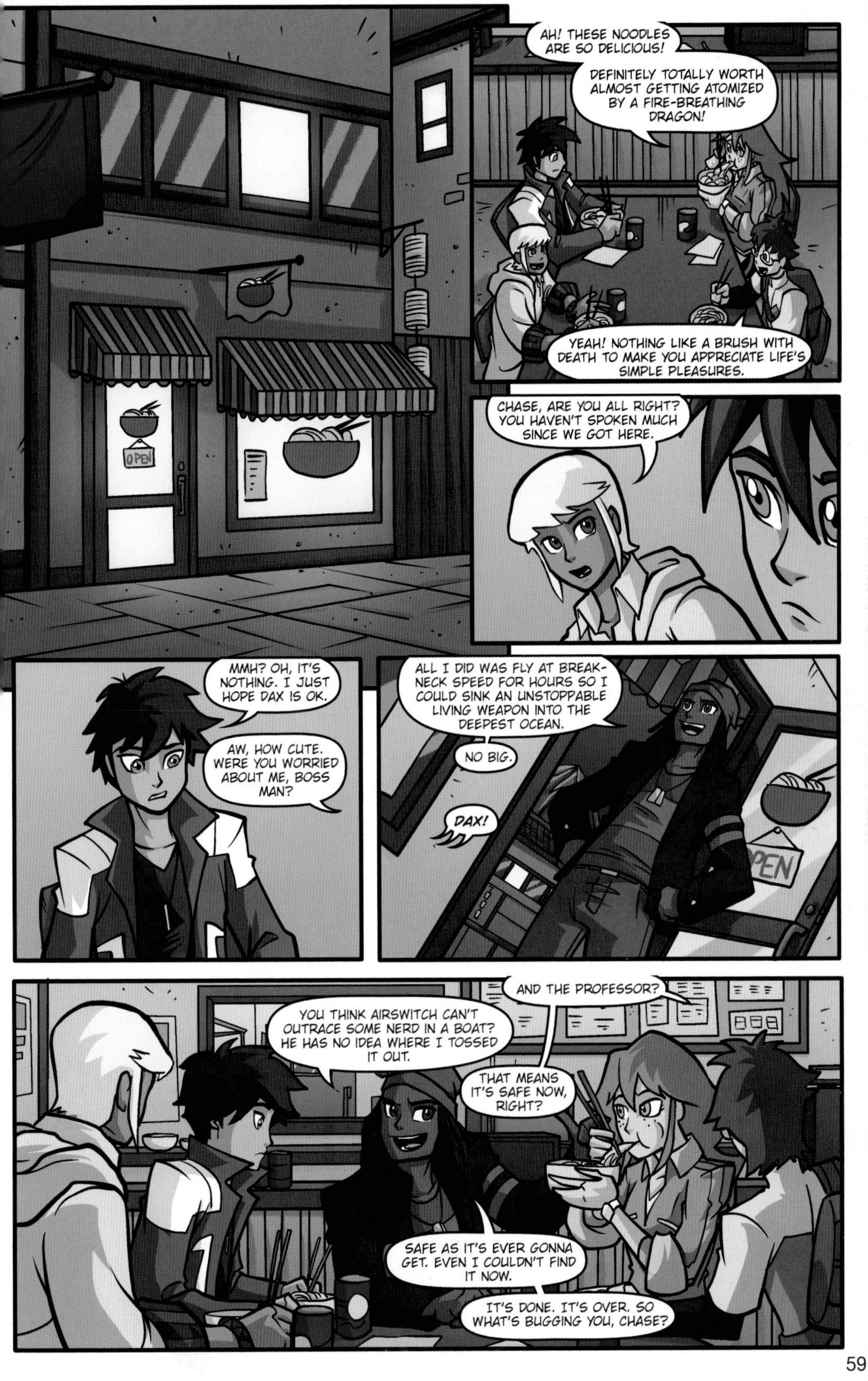
AH! THESE NOODLES ARE SO DELICIOUS!
DEFINITELY TOTALLY WORTH ALMOST GETTING ATOMIZED BY A FIRE-BREATHING DRAGON!
YEAH! NOTHING LIKE A BRUSH WITH DEATH TO MAKE YOU APPRECIATE LIFE'S SIMPLE PLEASURES.
CHASE, ARE YOU ALL RIGHT? YOU HAVEN'T SPOKEN MUCH SINCE WE GOT HERE.
MMH? OH, IT'S NOTHING. I JUST HOPE DAX IS OK.
AW, HOW CUTE. WERE YOU WORRIED ABOUT ME, BOSS MAN?
ALL I DID WAS FLY AT BREAK-NECK SPEED FOR HOURS SO I COULD SINK AN UNSTOPPABLE LIVING WEAPON INTO THE DEEPEST OCEAN.
NO BIG.
DAX!
AND THE PROFESSOR?
YOU THINK AIRSWITCH CAN'T OUTRACE SOME NERD IN A BOAT? HE HAS NO IDEA WHERE I TOSSED IT OUT.
THAT MEANS IT'S SAFE NOW, RIGHT?
SAFE AS IT'S EVER GONNA GET. EVEN I COULDN'T FIND IT NOW.
IT'S DONE. IT'S OVER. SO WHAT'S BUGGING YOU, CHASE?

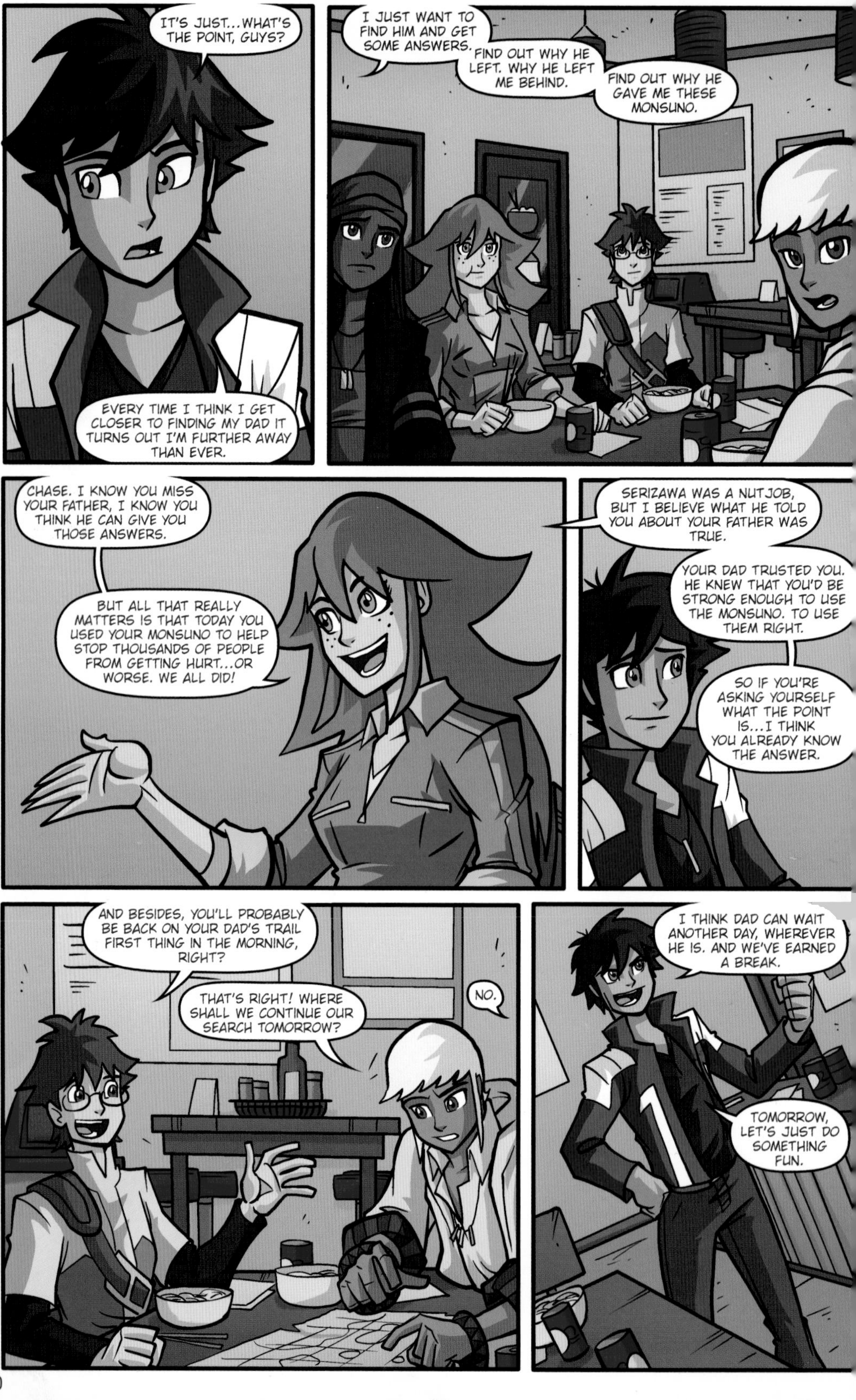
IT'S JUST...WHAT'S THE POINT, GUYS?
EVERY TIME I THINK I GET CLOSER TO FINDING MY DAD IT TURNS OUT I'M FURTHER AWAY THAN EVER.
I JUST WANT TO FIND HIM AND GET SOME ANSWERS.
FIND OUT WHY HE LEFT. WHY HE LEFT ME BEHIND.
FIND OUT WHY HE GAVE ME THESE MONSUNO.
CHASE. I KNOW YOU MISS YOUR FATHER, I KNOW YOU THINK HE CAN GIVE YOU THOSE ANSWERS.
BUT ALL THAT REALLY MATTERS IS THAT TODAY YOU USED YOUR MONSUNO TO HELP STOP THOUSANDS OF PEOPLE FROM GETTING HURT...OR WORSE. WE ALL DID!
SERIZAWA WAS A NUTJOB, BUT I BELIEVE WHAT HE TOLD YOU ABOUT YOUR FATHER WAS TRUE.
YOUR DAD TRUSTED YOU. HE KNEW THAT YOU'D BE STRONG ENOUGH TO USE THE MONSUNO. TO USE THEM RIGHT.
SO IF YOU'RE ASKING YOURSELF WHAT THE POINT IS...I THINK YOU ALREADY KNOW THE ANSWER.
AND BESIDES, YOU'LL PROBABLY BE BACK ON YOUR DAD'S TRAIL FIRST THING IN THE MORNING, RIGHT?
THAT'S RIGHT! WHERE SHALL WE CONTINUE OUR SEARCH TOMORROW?
NO.
I THINK DAD CAN WAIT ANOTHER DAY, WHEREVER HE IS. AND WE'VE EARNED A BREAK.
TOMORROW, LET'S JUST DO SOMETHING FUN.

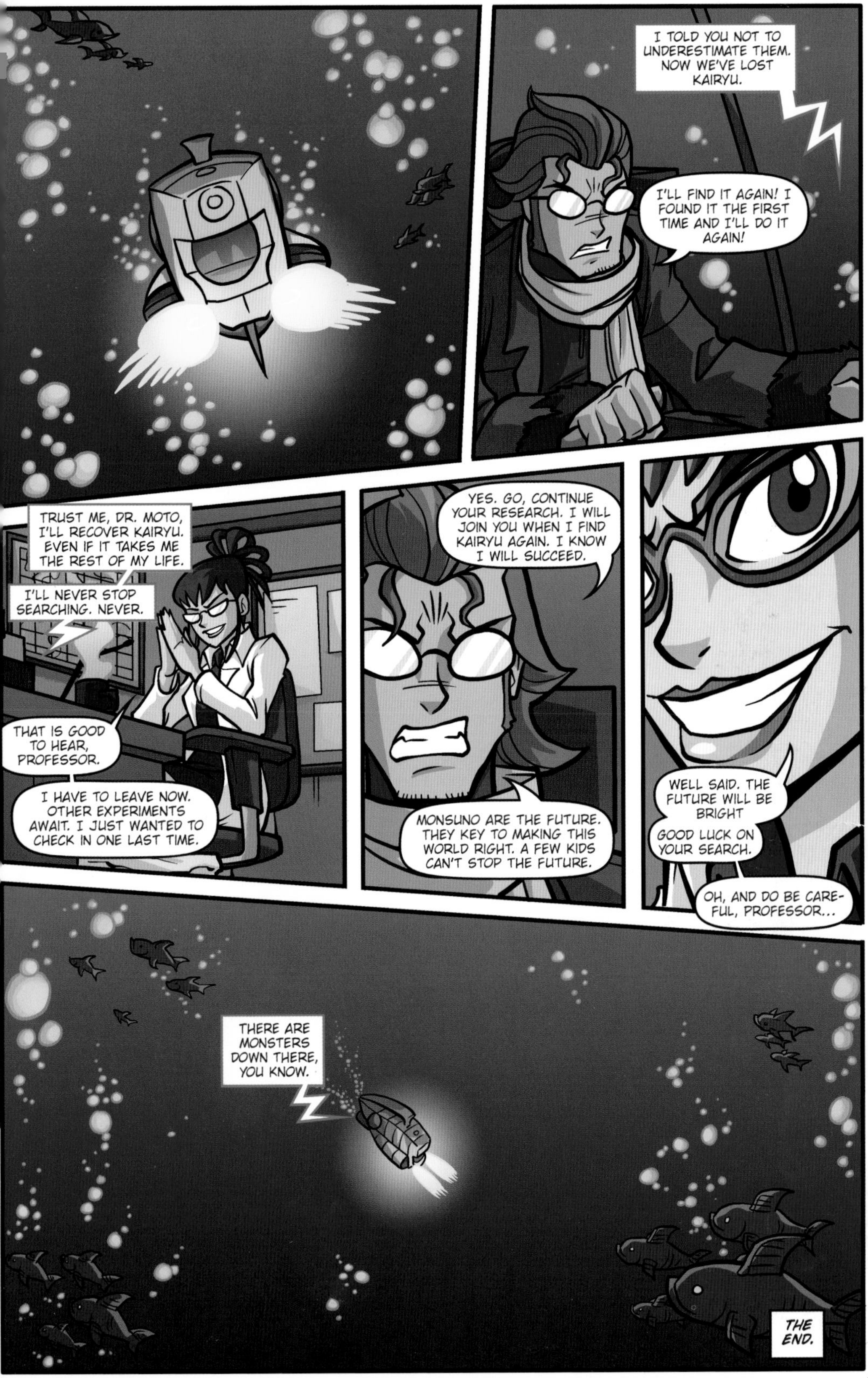
I TOLD YOU NOT TO UNDERESTIMATE THEM. NOW WE'VE LOST KAIRYU.
I'LL FIND IT AGAIN! I FOUND IT THE FIRST TIME AND I'LL DO IT AGAIN!
TRUST ME, DR. MOTO, I'LL RECOVER KAIRYU. EVEN IF IT TAKES ME THE REST OF MY LIFE.
I'LL NEVER STOP SEARCHING. NEVER.
THAT IS GOOD TO HEAR, PROFESSOR.
I HAVE TO LEAVE NOW. OTHER EXPERIMENTS AWAIT. I JUST WANTED TO CHECK IN ONE LAST TIME.
YES. GO, CONTINUE YOUR RESEARCH. I WILL JOIN YOU WHEN I FIND KAIRYU AGAIN. I KNOW I WILL SUCCEED.
MONSUNO ARE THE FUTURE. THEY KEY TO MAKING THIS WORLD RIGHT. A FEW KIDS CAN'T STOP THE FUTURE.
WELL SAID. THE FUTURE WILL BE BRIGHT
GOOD LUCK ON YOUR SEARCH.
OH, AND DO BE CARE-FUL, PROFESSOR...
THERE ARE MONSTERS DOWN THERE, YOU KNOW.
THE END.

WRITERS

SEBASTIAN GIRNER is a former editor for Marvel Entertainment, where he creatively guided such critically acclaimed series as *Punisher MAX*, *Fury MAX* and *Ghost Rider*. For Random House Publishing he translated and adapted manga, including *Bloody Monday* and *Cage of Eden*. Sebastian was born in Germany, raised in the US, has lived and studied in Japan and currently resides in New York City. His great passion is comics, no matter which country they are from.

ARTISTS

WRITE-HEIGHT MEDIA is a creative super-team-up of artist **RAY-ANTHONY HEIGHT**, who has penciled for *Spider-Man* and *Spider-Girl* (Marvel) and *Teenage Mutant Ninja Turtles* (Mirage), and artist **NATE LOVETT**, who has worked on *GI Joe*, *Star Wars* and *Mr. Potato Head* (Hasbro). Write-Height recently did pencils for *Redakai* (VIZ).

LETTERER/COLORIST

ZACK TURNER started out in the comics industry as an independent artist and colorist on *Unimaginable* (Arcana) and several projects for Bluewater. Recently he has been working on full art duties on *Redakai* (VIZ) as well as lettering *Max Steel* (VIZ).

MONSUNO

KAIRYU REDESIGN

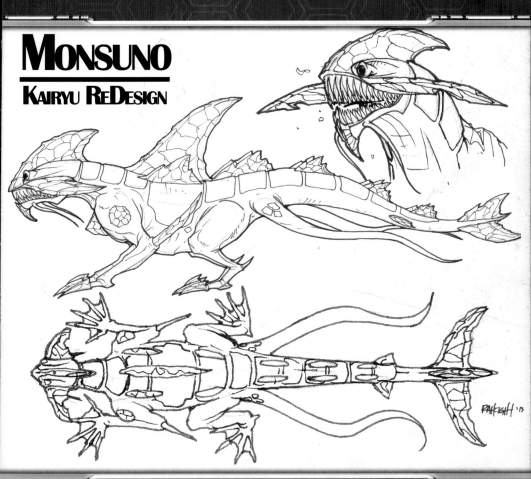

Early Kairyu designs by Ray-Anthony Height

COLLECT ALL THREE MONSUNO GRAPHIC NOVELS!

ON SALE NOW!

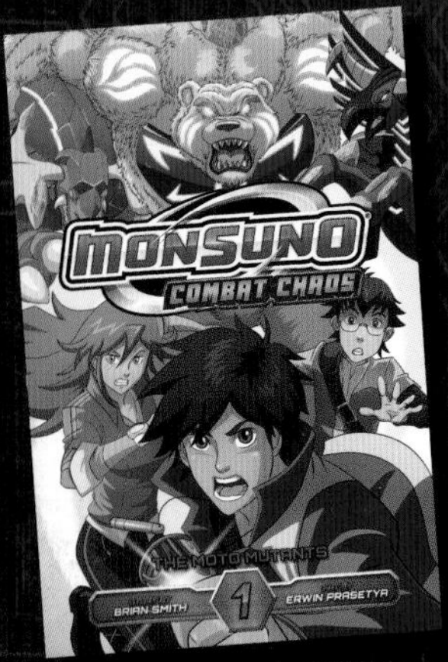
MONSUNO
COMBAT CHAOS
THE MOTO MUTANTS
BRIAN SMITH
1
ERWIN PRASETYA

Volume 1: THE MOTO MUTANTS

Long before Chase ever heard of Monsuno, scientists experimented with Monsuno essence. One such scientist, Dr. Moto, tried to create her own Monsuno, but her experiments went horribly wrong. Trapped in an icy lab, Dr. Moto has continued her terrible experiments for years, and now Chase, Bren and Jinja have stumbled upon her horrifying creations!

Volume 2: REVENGE/SACRIFICE

A traitor in Dr. Moto's ranks has Chase, Bren, Jinja and Dax in their clutches. Trapped in an underground lab with mutant Monsunos, our team must survive Dr. Moto's revenge! Plus, a new fierce battle brings back memories for Beyal about the past and Chase's missing dad, Jeredy Suno!

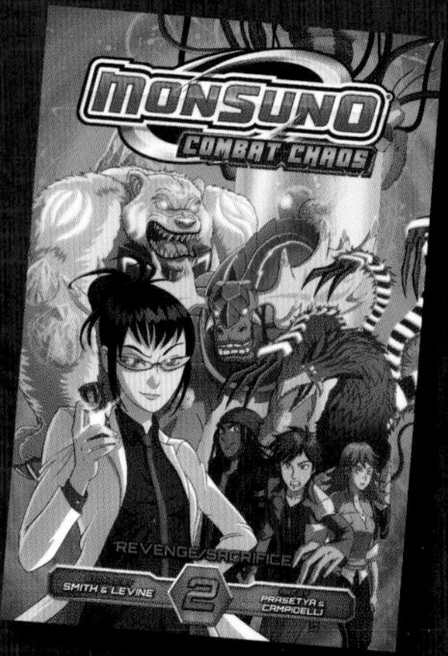
MONSUNO
COMBAT CHAOS
REVENGE/SACRIFICE
SMITH & LEVINE
2
PRASETYA & CAMPIDELLI

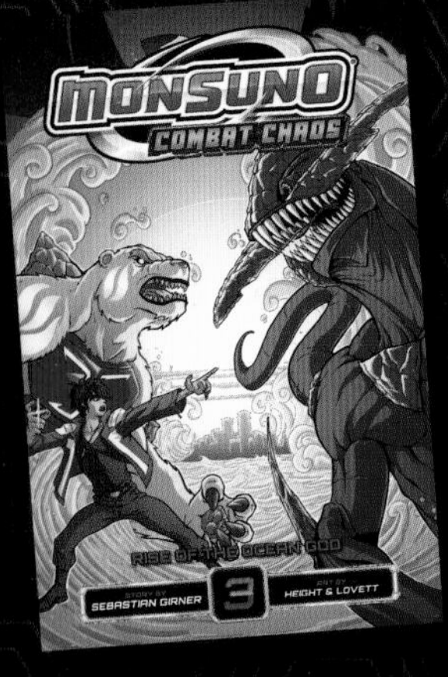
MONSUNO
COMBAT CHAOS
RISE OF THE OCEAN GOD
SEBASTIAN GIRNER
3
HEIGHT & LOVETT

Volume 3: RISE OF THE OCEAN GOD

Chase, Bren, Jinja and the others travel to a faraway island to find the mysterious Dr. Serizawa, who may have information about Chase's missing dad. Instead, they come face-to-face with an old enemy and an ancient secret that changes everything they think they know about the history of Monsuno on Earth...and puts the entire world in peril!